The Groundskeeper's
DAUGHTER

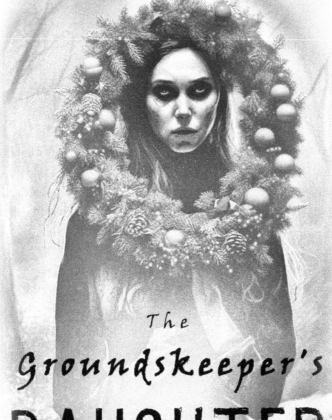

Copyright © 2024 Holly Knightley All rights reserved

This book is a work of fiction. Any references to historical events, real people, or real places are used fictitiously. Other names, characters, places, and events are products of the author's imagination, and any resemblance to actual events or places or persons, living or dead, is entirely coincidental.

No part of this book may be reproduced, or stored in a retrieval system, or transmitted in any form or by any means, electronic, mechanical, photocopying, recording, or otherwise, without express written permission of the publisher.

ISBN: 978-1-958761-62-5

Cover design: AW Rabbit Designs

*For Grandma and Grandpa Jackie
and my Uncle Johnny*

CONTENTS

CHAPTER ONE: *Godspeed* *1*

CHAPTER TWO: *An Early Christmas Gift* *8*

CHAPTER THREE: *Jay Smith* *12*

CHAPTER FOUR: *Reputation* *22*

CHAPTER FIVE: *The Figure in the Snow* *27*

CHAPTER SIX: *A Turn of Events* *37*

CHAPTER SEVEN: *His Molly* *49*

CHAPTER EIGHT: *A Visit* *64*

CHAPTER NINE: *A Bittersweet Christmas Eve* *73*

CHAPTER TEN: *A Full House* *90*

CHAPTER ONE

Godspeed

I wiped the cold sweat beading in my hairline with the back of my hand, taking a step back to admire my hard work. The snow left behind from the weekend's blizzard crested the top of the small gravestone like ice crystals, each flake seemingly visible as the sun cast its gaze upon it.

"Godspeed," I read from the tombstone with a deflated sigh. An hour and several blisters later, all I had to show for my labor was the message: Godspeed. I'd spent the better part of an hour meticulously cutting back two large boxwoods that most nurseries would have classified as small trees. These colossal waxy-leaved shrubs flanked what I knew had to be a headstone. I was in a cemetery after all. My father is the groundskeeper to Smith and Stone Cemetery and had been since I was born.

As a child, I would run through the aged headstones while other children ran through grass-ladened backyards. The hallowed grounds of the small private cemetery was my playground, that was until at eight years old, at the peak whimsy of my childhood, my parents got divorced and I moved with my mother to Mississippi. I only saw my father twice a year, three times on a good year.

My father had his right hip replaced at the beginning of the week and had no one there to care for him after the surgery. It was winter break, so I went. My mom wasn't pleased I was going to be spending Christmas away from home, but the last decade had been spent with her celebrating Christmas with a faux Christmas tree and a barbecue. It was time I came home to New Jersey for the holidays.

I missed the cold. I missed the snow. I missed Smith and Stone Cemetery, especially when it was blanketed in white. There's a magic here. I felt it when I was a little girl, and I felt it still as I looked out over the cemetery, the light playing tricks on my eyes, making it seem like millions of sugarplum fairies danced from one grave marker to the next.

The twinkling fairy lights brought my eyes back to the headstone I stood in front of. I was certain of the magic in this place where stones rose from the ground in unique shapes, cutting their own paths through the earth with the names of the dead carved into them like secrets. Secret stories the living will never be able to share in. Yes, there's magic at Smith and Stone Cemetery, but there's also sadness.

Like this particular headstone. The name of the deceased was lost to time. Everything about them was lost—their date of birth and death, any indication of who they were was erased by time's unyielding hand.

I loved the old stones that gave you a glimpse into the person buried under its stony shadow: mother, brother, soldier, beloved daughter, or son. This stone only sent a message: Godspeed, a farewell of good wishes as a new journey begins.

"Well," I said to the headstone as if I was speaking to the person it was placed for, "till next time, Godspeed."

I shoved my clippers inside one of the two large construction grade trash bags that were filled with boxwood clippings and dragged the bags toward the groundskeeper's cabin.

When I was a little girl, my mother would help my father care for Smith and Stone Cemetery. Come late November, she would clip the boxwoods throughout the grounds. Only the boxwoods. "You can clip them anytime of the year without risking killing them," she'd say to me every year as if one day it would be my job, but then I was merely tasked with collecting the clippings in a trash bag. Later, as a family, we would make miniature grave blankets to place on the forgotten graves to keep the dead warm for the holidays.

It sounds a little macabre or maybe strange, but I always thought it was sweet. My father was the groundskeeper after all and I, his daughter. We were the caretakers of the dead and I took pride in it. This pride renewed as I pulled my two large trash bags of boxwoods into the house.

The groundskeeper's cottage was built in the late 1700's and as what was to be expected, was small with a cramped layout. The eat-in kitchen smacked you in the face as soon as you walked in, but it was homey, and I loved seeing the large timbers that ran across the kitchen. The original brick fireplace with a rustic timber mantle was still in the home, but we did have to put a cast iron stove inside the fireplace to update the cottage to the fire code. No charm was lost in doing so and the old pot belly stove that currently roared with a fire made the place feel like you were living in a story book. The live tree was in the corner waiting for me to decorate it with my late grandmother's famous Christmas gingerbread that the birds go wild for after the holidays.

The groundskeeper's cabin was just the right size for a small, loving family. And that's how it was for me growing up. To be back in this place, smelling the old wood and soot, the smell of damp earth and stone clinging to my nose like a forgotten memory, made me feel like a little girl again. I knew this was going to be the best Christmas I had in a long time.

"Hi dad," I said, happy to see him sitting at the kitchen table with his leg elevated as his doctor had ordered. He was skimming the newspaper and put it down at the sound of me coming in.

"Hey Mol, what do you have there?"

"Tons of boxwood clippings to make grave blankets."

"Good," he said, "with my hip, I didn't think it was going to get done this year."

The red blotches dabbling his cheeks let me know this family tradition ended when my mother and I left, which I had assumed. I asked him every year for a picture of the cemetery after it snowed, and he never sent one. I had always suspected he didn't want to incriminate himself and now I knew for sure.

"Don't worry, we still have five days to get these puppies made. But, um, Dad, on the other side of the cottage there was one grave that was really overgrown. Do you know the one I'm talking about? Who's buried there?"

His eyes narrowed.

"Well not that overgrown," I added quickly.

My father was sensitive about the state of the cemetery. It was in need of some TLC. In truth, it had always been too large for him to manage by himself and with his double knee replacement in the summer and now his hip, the grounds suffered. The Boy Scouts used to come and help, putting the flags out for Memorial Day and cutting the grass in the summer, but the contract with them ended years ago and he had no help since. Being privately owned, there was no allowance to hire anyone. The Smith's hired my father and if he couldn't do it, they'd find someone else.

"Well?" I asked, knowing there was a good chance my father would know who was buried under the mystery Godspeed headstone. He was an encyclopedia of names, well—of Smith and Stone Cemetery residence. Before the modern computer system, my father was the computer. Him, and what he called the grave bible, a book of who was buried where, were the data base. Thanks to sites like Ancestory.com, people came to Smith and Stone Cemetery more than ever to hunt for long lost relatives. My father knew the graveyard inside and out. Even if the Smiths could find someone better suited at the manual labor aspect of being a groundskeeper, they'd never find a walking map like my father.

"Are you talking about Old James?"

"I don't know," I said with a shrug. "The name is totally worn away. It was the one between the two huge boxwoods, which I should add look like bonsai trees now." I beamed, thinking of the newly trimmed boxwoods and how nice they looked.

"Please tell me you didn't get those," he said, pointing at the trash bags by the door, his voice laced with what came off as anger, "from old James's grave."

You would've thought I just dragged in trash bags of skulls I'd dug up from the cemetery. "I nibbled on the inside of my cheek; I had this feeling I was in trouble. "Maybe."

"Molly, you know you're not supposed to touch that grave. Order of the Smith family. That grave has never been maintained in all the years it's been there and is never to be."

"Uh, no, I didn't know that. I didn't even recall there being a grave on the other side of the cottage." I'm sure as a child I must've thought it was merely a shrub, not having the common sense to know a gravestone was between the two large boxwoods. "Why? What's the big deal?"

My father shifted in his chair; both his feet planted on the ground now. He steepled his fingers on the worn kitchen table. I had never seen my father so serious. He was the goofy kind of dad. The dad who dressed up for Halloween and came to class parties and sang happy birthday over the phone every year despite you not being a little girl anymore. "I was told when I took the job, not to take care of that headstone under any circumstances. So, I never did. I abandoned it. It was behind the cabin, so even back when this place looked better, it wasn't an eyesore, and I just let it be."

I took a seat across from my father at the kitchen table. "Well, thanks to Old James we'll have plenty of grave blankets this year," I said cheerfully, trying to snap my dad out of his current mood.

"Don't you be putting one on Old James," my father said, his tone sounding more like a warning than anything else now. "He's not to be cared for."

"Not even on Christmas?"

"Especially not on Christmas."

I felt like I was dealing with Ebenezer Scrooge. I reduced my eyes to slits, giving him the look my mother always gave me and I knew she gave him before the divorce. "And you don't know why?"

"It's just cemetery lore. Mr. Foley didn't know. Just said it's how it's always been and it's best not to disturb the dead with change. Some souls have a hard time resting in the bed they made for themselves, and Old James has been known to be restless this time of year. Mr. Foley told me as much and I'm to tell the next groundskeeper the same." He ran his hand through his gray hair. I wasn't sure but it looked like his hand was trembling. "Clippings from old James's grave . . . Mr. Foley, God rest his soul, would be rolling over in his grave."

"Sorry Dad, I didn't know."

I was sure he was upset because he was worried about being fired. I knew he'd been worried about that for some time. He had hinted at it to my mother, and she had told me. With the grounds looking less than mediocre, and with the *do-not-disturb* grave very much disturbed, I figured the Smiths would have plausible cause to fire my father. I had no idea how often the Smiths came to check on my dad, but figured with Christmas less than a week away, they wouldn't be stopping by. I was here for a month and that would give me time to get everything looking nice before I went back to Mississippi.

"I won't put a grave blanket on Old James."

The front door swung open; a gust of wind whipped through the house in a howl, sending a chill down my spine. It was different than the chill you get from the cold, it lingered, penetrating deep into my bones and making my entire person ache. I shook out like a wet dog before running to the front door and closing it. This time I made sure the old lock caught.

"Nothing like the cold weather to put you in the Christmas spirit," I said with an unsure smile in my father's direction.

CHAPTER TWO
An Early Christmas Gift

The cemetery's magic was palpable in the morning. Jack Frost had paid a special visit to us in the middle of the night, painting the windows of the cottage with Christmas scenes and the same for the sparkling grounds that stretched out before me like cresting white waves.

I breathed in the fresh morning air, the cold stinging my lungs in a good way. I couldn't remember the last time I voluntarily woke up this early. As a girl, winter morns at Smith and Stone Cemetery were always my favorite. The hustle and bustle of the busy street was a dull murmur in the quiet of the morning. The sound of car stereos and beeping horns were traded in for the soft calls of birds.

I was already thinking I'd come back to Smith and Stone Cemetery for Christmas next year as I took my first step into the snow, my feet crunching through the thin layer of ice covering it.

I had a busy day ahead of me. My game plan was to distribute the grave blankets my father and I made last night and then it was back to the cottage to bake cookies while my father went to physical therapy.

Last night was a lot of fun, once my father stopped worrying about Old James. It was just how it was when I was a little girl. My father was all thumbs when it came to arts and crafts, needing my help like I was the adult and he was the child. But I didn't mind. That was how it was when I was eight and having the present recall me to my childhood made my belly feel warm and fuzzy with the Christmas spirit.

We had made a night of it. With the cuttings from Old James's boxwoods, we made grave blankets in the shape of a wreath. They were small, about eight inches in diameter, but our goal was to blanket as much of the dead for Christmas as we could.

I had bought some curling ribbon and miniature Christmas balls at the dollar store. Each boxwood wreath received two glitter balls and a bow. They looked really nice for my college student budget.

Blissfully coasting down nostalgia lane, I placed the homemade grave blankets on the graves that had been special to me when I was a child. In no time, I was down to my last wreath. I looked around the grounds; there were so many forgotten graves. Smith and Stone Cemetery was an old cemetery, most of its residents being buried between the 1700-1800's. Only a few families still came to place grave blankets on the long ago deceased. There was a newer section, though it looked just as scanty.

I glanced down at my last wreath, my numb hands gripping it like it was a steering wheel, "To whom shall you go?"

I'm not sure why, but I looked back to the cottage, Old James's headstone a dark smudge on the horizon. I knew, despite promising my father I wouldn't put a grave blanket on Old James, this last wreath was for him. No one should be forgotten, and he had been for so long. It was Christmas, it was a time for forgiveness, right? His headstone had already been upkept; the damage was done. I couldn't see the harm in placing the grave blanket. This wreath would be a physical gesture of what his headstone said:

Godspeed. I hoped this wreath would comfort him on his next journey, knowing not everyone had forgotten about him.

***

I headed back toward the cottage. I left the empty trash bag by the front door and made my way around the back of the cottage to Old James. It sounded like my feet were eating cereal as they crunched through the layer of ice over the snow, each step louder than the next.

Abruptly, I stopped, my breath funneling out of my mouth like a train, twirling in front of my eyes before disappearing. On the ground, in front of Old James's headstone was a bookmark with my name embroidered on it. I picked it up, running my gloved hand over the blue stitching that spelled out the letters of my name.

Again, I found myself looking at Old James's headstone as if it was a face. My pulse quickened, but I wasn't scared. Not really. This was something nice, this was a gift. "Where did you get this? I lost this a long, long time ago." It was true. I had made a bookmark just like the one I held when I was in second grade. It was exactly like it down to the small blue flowers on each corner.

At school, the last period every Friday was used for creative enrichment, having each student put in a group to work on a project. I had requested to learn embroidery and had worked on making my bookmark all year. At the end of the school year, I got to take it home. I was so proud of myself when I ran to show my mother what I had made, but when I opened my hand to show her my bookmark, it was gone. In my excitement, I had somehow dropped it.

My mother and I scoured the school hallways for it. I was the only Molly in the school. The name wasn't as popular as it is now, not that it's popular. Despite my mother's efforts, we came up empty handed. It was never turned into lost and found. I cried and I cried for days afterwards, mourning the loss of my bookmark like a dead friend. I couldn't understand why someone would want a bookmark with someone else's name on it.

I turned the bookmark around to examine it. Surely this couldn't be *my* bookmark. That's impossible. I had lost it over ten years ago. It had happened right before my parents got divorced. I had cried for my bookmark, and I had cried for my parents and for myself.

Yet, something told me it was *my* bookmark. It was obviously made by a child. You could tell it was a child's attempt at something grand, the stitches being of varied lengths and tautness; even so, it was charming and lovely in only the way things made by children can be.

To have my bookmark in my hand again was beyond surreal. The feeling that spread from my chest to my arms was a hot flush that consumed me with what I could only pinpoint as a deep gratefulness.

"Thank you," I said, hoping wherever Old James was he heard me. "I have something for you too." I placed the last homemade grave blanket on the ground where my bookmark had been moments ago. "I didn't forget about you James."

CHAPTER THREE
Jay Smith

My father had just left to go to therapy when I heard a knock on the door. Thinking my father had forgotten something and was now going to be late for his physical therapy appointment, I rushed to the front door, not taking the time to wash the cookie dough off my fingers. I opened the door with my thumb and pinky, doing my best not to leave smudges on the doorknob.

I found myself speechless at the well-dressed young man smiling at me. He was handsome in the way few men are. He was proof faeries were living amongst us. He had an otherworldly look to him. I was sure this was largely due to his beautiful violet-tinted gray eyes. His hair was dark auburn. He wasn't a true red head but there were shades of red in his brown hair that were highlighted thanks to the sun radiating from behind him. His fair skin looked like it should be dabbled with freckles, but it wasn't. It was flawless. Again, I thought Fae. Maybe he was one of the faeries that danced atop the snow-covered gravestones, here to take me away to Fairyland where I would live out the rest of my life as a princess.

Before I could formulate a thought that wouldn't usher me to an insane asylum, he introduced himself. "Hi, sorry to bother you. My name is Jay Smith, my family owns the cemetery."

I could feel my face physically droop as if he just spit acid at me and I was melting. "You're here to fire my father," rushed out of my mouth. Tears already stung the back of my throat as I swallowed to keep them down. My father was getting fired and it was all my fault.

"What?! No," he said, wrinkling his face as if it was me who had spit acid at him. "I don't have that kind of authority. And even if I did, I wouldn't. The place looks picturesque, like a Hallmark card with the snow and all of the wreaths on the graves. It's just how it looked when I was a boy."

I felt a tear spill over. I wiped it, knowing I just smeared cookie on my face.

"Seriously," he said, pulling out his phone. "I'm not here to fire anyone. Sure, it's a family-owned cemetery, but I have no part in who stays and who goes, my brother does. I design headstones and monuments."

He flashed a few images at me, swiping through his phone blind as I looked at the carousel of well-designed headstones. I was impressed, but I wasn't going to say so.

"I wasn't looking for your father, I was looking for you. You're Molly Delray, right?"

I corked an eyebrow. "Uh, yeah."

Sliding his phone back in his pocket, he looked past me, tilting his chin up. "Something's burning."

I sniffed in, smelling the smoke for the first time. I ran back to the kitchen and threw open the oven door. Black smoke filled the cramped space. Jay rushed in to help me, throwing up the sash to the window above the sink.

"They're ruined," I said, placing the tray of blackened gingerbread men on the stovetop. Not even the birds would eat these. It was a total waste.

THE GROUNDSKEEPER'S DAUGHTER

My eyes fell on the reason for my burnt gingerbread men—Jay Smith. He stood in my kitchen, fanning smoke out the window with his cashmere scarf.

"You were looking for me," I said in a leading way. If he wasn't here to fire my father, why was he here?

Jay obnoxiously cleared his throat, whether it was because of the dose of carcinogens we just inhaled or because he felt awkward, I wasn't sure. "Um, yeah," he said, yet again clearing his throat. "I found this." I watched him dig through his coat pockets, before pulling something from one of them and handing it to me.

"My license," I said dumbstruck.

"I found it and thought you might want it back. Going to the DMV is a nightmare this time of year."

"Thanks, but you didn't have to. I already got a new one," I said, scanning over the familiar picture of myself, my eyes grazing over my Mississippi address: Twenty-five Peanut Brittle Lane, Starkville, MS. The tiny hairs on my arms stood on end as if I'd just stuck my finger in an electrical outlet. I was on full alert. My heart thudding away in my chest.

"Where did you say you found it again?" He didn't, but I wanted to know. I lost my license months ago while at home in Mississippi. How did Jay Smith come to find it? This was the strangest thing that ever happened to me, well besides my lost bookmark showing up after a decade of heartache.

Jay rubbed the back of his neck, "On the ground, on the sidewalk, down the street."

Jay was lucky he was cute because he was awkward. It didn't help he wore his feelings. He was nervous. So nervous, I was worried he was going to rub the skin off the nape of his neck. His anxiety was making me anxious. There was no way he found my license in Bloomfield or any street in Jersey. He was lying and I wanted to know why. More than that, I wanted him to leave. He knew who I was, how else did he know to find me at my father's house, but how did I know if he was who he said *he* was? Because he showed me pictures of tombstones on his phone? If anything, that should raise a red flag, and this guy was in my kitchen.

I glanced at the clock on the wall. My father wouldn't be home for an hour. "Well thanks for dropping my license off," I said, making my way to the open front door as a means to hint it was time for him to leave.

Instead of following me to the door, Jay took off his coat, hanging it on the back of a kitchen chair before taking a seat. "Good idea, I think you can close the door now, most of the smoke is out. So uh, do you have any cookies without peanuts that aren't burnt?"

I shut the door and came back into the kitchen. He smiled at me as if he expected me to laugh. I didn't, but I faked a smile. "I only have gingerbread."

"Great, I love gingerbread."

I took a few cookies off the cooling rack and placed them on a plate in front of him.

"Thanks," he said, taking one. "You have anything to drink?"

"Water, milk, or eggnog?"

"Eggnog, please." I opened the refrigerator door, discreetly looking for my cell phone in case I needed to dial for help." I spotted it next to the sink.

I took a Christmas mug out of the cupboard, tucking my cell phone into my apron before pouring Jay a glass of eggnog and placing it alongside the plate of cookies.

"Wow, this is good," he said, taking a sip. "Did you make it?"

I nodded, keeping my distance from him and resting my back against the sink, my hand in my apron clutching my phone, ready. "So, you're a member of the Smith family . . ."

"Yep," he said, dunking his gingerbread man into his eggnog.

"So that means you know all about Old James?"

At mention of Old James, his hand jerked violently, knocking his mug over. The thick drink painted the tabletop yellow before dripping on to the floor. *At least the mug didn't break.*

Before the eggnog could drip on him, Jay shot up, giving a jolt to the table that sent the mug crashing to the floor.

The sound of it shattering made me suck air.

"I'm sorry!" He said, his hands reaching toward the sky like he just got caught robbing a bank.

"Spoke too early," I muttered to myself, throwing paper towels over the mess on the table and floor.

"Geez, I'm really sorry. I'm such a klutz. I'll replace it." He was back to rubbing the nape of his neck.

"It's fine, this table has seen worse than eggnog and you don't have to replace the mug."

He may have made a mess, but there was a silver lining to losing my cat Christmas mug. I believed he was who he said he was. Jay knew exactly who I was talking about when I said Old James. His reaction to Old James was stronger than my father's, which was to be expected if he was a Smith.

Jay settled back into his seat as I threw the last of the mess in the trash.

"Let's try this again," I said with a kind smile, pouring him a new cup of eggnog. I went with a chipped mug just in case he really was accident prone, and his blunder had nothing to do with the mentioning of Old James.

With my own cup of eggnog, I took a seat across from Jay. After finding my bookmark this morning, I did a quick Google search on Old James and turned up nothing useful. James Smith is the most common first and last name combo in America. And what I *could* find was all about James Smith, the founder of Smith and Stone Cemetery. Old James was not this James. Founder of Smith and Stone Cemetery, James Smith, at one time was the wealthiest man in the state, having developed land for cemeteries. The Revolutionary War and Civil War proved this a wise investment. I confirmed Founder James Smith had a son named James Smith and that was about it.

While I had Jay here, I was going to get some answers. There was this gap in who Old James was perceived to be and who he was. He was a man who was supposed to be forgotten but he had shown me a kindness finding my bookmark. Why was my father's reaction to him negative and Jay's reaction, if I had to guess—scared?

I knew I should probably be more freaked out about the bookmark showing up out of the blue, but I wasn't. I was brought up on the belief the dead can't hurt you, only the living can. Which was a good thing to believe when you grow up in a cemetery.

"Can I ask you a question?" I asked, taking notice of Jay's rosy cheeks after the mishap with the eggnog. His blush made him look much younger than he was.

He lifted his eyes to me, his dark hair falling over his temples, emphasizing the flecks of purple in his eyes. "Yeah . . ."

"What's Old James's story? Why does the mention of his name make my dad angry and you jittery? And why can't anyone care for his grave?"

Jay leaned back in his chair, taking in a large gulp of air. "That was three questions," he said with a sideways grin, "but I'll tell you. It's why I'm here after all."

My eyes narrowed in intrigue. "You're here because of Old James?" My mind went to my found license. Had Old James found it? If so, why give it to Jay and not to me?

"Old James was the oldest of the three James brothers."

"So, Old James is just the oldest, not that he was old?"

"Yeah, my family has this tradition of naming all the males in the family James. My birth certificate reads James Smith, but I go by Jay. My father went by Jim, my eldest brother, Jimmy, and my youngest brother goes by John."

"That's bizarre," I said fascinated. I've heard of first-born sons being named after their father. I even have a few friends who are juniors but naming all the boys in every generation the same name seemed crazier than my bookmark and license being returned to me.

"Not that bizarre. The famous boxer, George Foreman, named all five of his sons George Foreman."

"Sticking with my gut reaction on this one. It's weird."

The corners of his lips twisted up. "Okay, I'll admit it's a little weird. It's a Druid thing that goes way back. It's been that way forever and since the family has enough bad luck as it comes, no one wanted to break the tradition. My younger brother John always said he'd be the first, but he named his two sons James, and he has another one on the way, that's also going to be named James. Not that anyone goes by their birthname. No one does because of Old James."

I was just about to ask why that was when Jay let out a stressed laugh. "Funny enough, that's another thing we all have in common. Going all the way back to my great-great-great, who knows how many greats, great grandfather. He was the youngest of his three brothers and the only one to have children. The same went for all of my great grandfathers, and grandfather. My father was also the youngest and he had three boys, and my brother John is following the same pattern."

"You're joking."

"No joke. Not only do we all share the same name and have

two brothers, we all have a peanut allergy, gray eyes, and will die at the age of twenty-five on Christmas."

I tilted my head in thought. "So, you're telling me . . ."

"I'm going to die in four days. I turned twenty-five three weeks ago. It's my year."

This sounded nuts but he seemed earnest, like not only was he telling the truth, but he was sharing it for the first time. "How can you possibly know that? And what does it have to do with Old James?"

He pushed his dark hair away from his face. "It's how it's always been. It's how Old James made it. My brothers and I didn't grow up knowing. It was my father's wish that we, like him and his brothers, were told at eighteen. That way we could have normal childhoods. We all dealt with the news differently. My older brother Jimmy turned to drugs. John married his high school sweetheart as soon as they graduated high school and started a family. I wanted to leave a mark on the world and decided to design headstones and monuments and anything else made from stone. That way, when I'm gone, my work will still be out there. I designed a really nice headstone for Jimmy and myself. I couldn't bring myself to design one for John. I hope he can break the curse for his kids' sake."

Jay's gray eyes turned glassy at the mention of his brothers. I put my hand on his, it was trembling. "What curse?" I said in a whisper, not sure why I dropped my voice. But the house had grown somber; I couldn't hear the street traffic, or the wind outside, or the birds. It was just Jay and me.

"Old James cursed the family when he died. His death was not a normal death. He died at twenty-five." Jay shook his head at himself. "That's not right, he was murdered at twenty-five by his father."

My eyes grew wide. Jay paused, leaning his head back to stop the tears from rolling down his face. My hand slipped into his.

"Why would his father murder him?"

"He murdered his eldest son to deliver his own justice. You see, Old James killed his younger brother who was fifteen at the time. My grandfather was a baby when it happened and passed down only what was told to him by his mother, so the facts are blurry. All I know for sure is that Old James killed his brother on Christmas, and in turn his father killed him. And in four days, Old James will kill me."

"This doesn't make sense; Old James is nice."

Jay ripped his hand from mine to point out the window at the Smith family obelisk in the center of the cemetery. His eyes burned with a violet flame. "You think it's nice that he murdered my father and left him face down in the cemetery Christmas morning! You think it's nice that he scared my brother into developing an opioid addiction to handle it all, just to end up dead in his car on Christmas!"

"I'm sorry, I didn't mean to make you upset, it's just that I think I've made contact with Old James, and he seems friendly."

Jay's tone softened, his cheeks alive with a cranberry flush. "Trust me, he's not Casper the friendly ghost. He killed my father and my brother and every other male in the family." He looked back toward the cemetery. "The thought that he's going to kill my nephews one day is more than I can bear. Maybe it's a good thing I only have four days left."

"Don't talk like that."

His purple-tinted eyes landed on me. "Wait, Old James made contact with you?!" He asked alarmed. "Did he hurt you?"

"He found my bookmark. I'm sure it was him. I kinda did some upkeeping on his plot, not knowing I wasn't supposed to touch it."

He nodded. "It was him. That's how I found your license. I

woke up this morning and there it was on my nightstand and my laptop was opened to your social media post of the cemetery. It's how I knew where to find you." He looked to the ceiling, as if in thought. "It's all making sense now."

"What is? Why would he give you my license?"

"This is how it started for Jimmy, the beginning of the end that is. Before Jimmy died, he started talking to this strange girl, taking her calls in private."

"Who was she?"

"No one knows. When he died a few days later, no one unknown to the family came to the funeral. I don't know who she was or what her business with my brother was, but I'm thinking Old James brought them together, like he brought us together."

"That *does* make sense. I think I'm supposed to help you break the curse."

"I shouldn't have come here," Jay said, getting up. "I have no right to drag you into my personal shit storm. You seem nice Molly, too nice. I don't want you getting hurt. Who knows what happened to the girl Jimmy was talking to. There could be a reason she didn't come to his funeral. She could've ended up dead too. I didn't know what to expect when I knocked on your door, but now that I've met you, I'm not going to endanger you."

I stood, trying to make myself come off more assertive, my hand gripping his to show I meant business. "And I'm not going to abandon you. We're in this together, whether you like it or not."

CHAPTER FOUR
Reputation

Jay and I both jumped at the sound of the keys rattling the lock to the front door. "My father's home," I said as our hands mutually pulled apart, the intense moment shared between us lost.

I opened the door for my father so he wouldn't have to struggle with his walker. "Hey Dad, how was therapy?" I rubbed my fingers together; Jay's touch still tingled my skin. There was just something about him.

"Hello Mr. Delray," Jay said.

My father shook Jay's hand. "Jay, I didn't know you were stopping by. And for the last time it's Al."

"Uh, yeah, sorry. I should've called ahead. I just figured with the hip you'd be home. I wanted to drop off your Christmas card. He reached for his coat, pulling it off the chair to fish out two cards. "The other's from my mother with the um," his eyelids fluttered as he looked down. "It's from my mother."

"Thank you," my father said, taking the cards from him.

I watched my father slip the cards into his coat pocket before hanging his coat on the hook by the side of the door. I found it odd he didn't open the Christmas cards in front of Jay.

Jay put on his coat, tying his scarf around his neck. "You

have a lovely daughter Al, and her cookies aren't half bad," he said with a half grin in my direction. The grin melted my heart; it showed off his dimples. "Well, I should get going, I've got lots of errands to run today."

"I'll see you tomorrow," I said in a rushed voice.

His eyes danced to mine, holding me in the frame of his dark lashes. "Okay."

"Early. Meet me here for eight in the morning."

"Eight, got it," he said. He shook my father's hand again, turning to me. "Thanks for the cookies Molly and sorry again about the mug. See you tomorrow, early."

* * *

"What was that about?" My father said, making his way to the kitchen table.

I tarried by the front door, watching out the window as Jay made his way through the cemetery. "What was what about?"

"How long was Jay here?"

I didn't like lying to my father, but this was one of those situations that warranted a lie. He was already way too uptight over Old James; he didn't need to know Jay was here because of him. "Not long. He said he had something for you, and I said he could wait inside, that you would be home any minute."

"He said he liked your cookies. It sounds like he was here longer than a few minutes."

"No not really. While he waited, I offered him a gingerbread man."

"And what was that about a mug?"

"I also offered him some eggnog and he dropped the mug and broke it."

"I don't see the mess."

"I cleaned it up, Dad," I said, my eyes focusing in on him

like a spider moving toward its prey. "What's up with the third degree?"

"I don't want you hanging around Jay Smith."

I could feel my facial features twist in confusion. I hate it when I can feel it happening. It's like I'm morphing into some unknown beast. "You seemed pretty chummy with him a moment ago."

"He's my boss."

"I don't know, I thought Jay was nice."

"He's not." My father shook his head. "He's bad news, stay away from him."

I wondered if my father knew about the Smith curse. Had Mr. Foley told him? It would explain his reaction to me trimming the boxwoods around Old James's headstone. I should've come straight out and asked him, but I didn't want to add more fuel to the fire. If he didn't want me hanging out with Jay before, he'd make sure of it after learning about the curse.

"No offense Dad, but I'm eighteen, you can't tell me who I can and cannot hang out with."

He ran his hand through his dark hair that was salted in gray. I looked a lot like my father. We had the same dark hair and eyes. The kind of eyes that look like blackholes, nothing like Jay's expressive eyes that twinkled like the heavens. "I've known Jay all his life. I'm good friends with his mother and well, Jay has a bad reputation when it comes to women, and I don't want you near him. I know you're not a little girl anymore, but I'm your father and it's my duty to protect you."

Jay was by far the best-looking man I'd seen in real life; he could definitely give Hollywood a run for its money, of course he had a reputation when it came to women. I was sure Jay Smith of the Smith and Stone empire had multiple girlfriends in different states, maybe even different countries. He was handsome and filthy rich; those two things tend to attract trouble.

I caught a glimpse of myself in the mirror by the front door and flushed. I had forgotten all about the cookie dough I wiped on my face when I answered the knock on the front door. Somehow, I managed to streak flour across my cheek and got some in my dark hair. Jay probably thought I was prematurely going gray. And my worse offense, a blob of cookie dough clung to my chin like a witch's wort.

My instant attraction to Jay embarrassed me. I felt silly and ugly, and oh so silly. A guy like Jay could never find me pretty, not when I looked like the witch from *Hansel and Gretel*.

I wiped off my cookie dough wort on my apron. "A reputation? What do you mean?" I asked, looking for a little clarity. Despite not having a chance with Jay, I was curious. I wanted to know if he was married, divorced, or had a steady girlfriend. I was sure I could find that out online, but with my dad being friends with his mother, he may have inside dirt.

"It's not a good one Mol. He doesn't treat women with respect."

My father's rosy cheeks were a few shades redder than they had been when he came in from the cold, confirming he meant Jay was sexually promiscuous. I could understand why he didn't want his only daughter hanging around with a scoundrel that he thought would steal her virginity in the middle of the night like a wolf going after a lamb. But there might be more to it than that.

Jay had seemed really nice, but he had raised his voice at me. I knew it was out of frustration but still, maybe my father was right, and he was someone I was better off avoiding. Yet, there was this tiny burning feeling deep in my core, like a bad case of indigestion, that let me know I couldn't just walk away from Jay and his problem. There was something there. I cared what happened to him, which was crazy. I just met him.

I glanced out the window, wanting to look at Jay one last time to make sure I judged him right. He stood in front of the Smith monument, the resting place of Founder James and his family. If I believed everything he told me, the place where his father was found dead. Jay's darkened form stood out amongst the snow-covered graves like he was a fresh headstone. The thought chilled me.

My father was overreacting. As long as Jay didn't kill women to wear their skin, I'd be okay. Besides, I was positive Jay wasn't looking at me like that. He didn't choose to knock on my door. Old James chose me. And as nuts as it was, I chose to help Jay.

CHAPTER FIVE

The Figure in the Snow

I'm usually a heavy sleeper, when I'm out, I'm out. I've been known to sleep through my alarm on more than one occasion. Yet, I found myself tossing and turning, rerunning the day through my head. "The dead can't hurt the living," I muttered to myself. But I fact checked everything Jay had told me. I found his brother's obituary straight away. He *had* died last Christmas, and his father had also died on Christmas over a decade ago, like he'd said.

Old James wasn't some kind spirit helping the living find things they misplaced. He was a poltergeist with a plan and that plan seemed to end with the death of a Smith. This year's unlucky victim —Jay.

It just didn't make sense to me. How could a ghost kill you and why would it want to? Notwithstanding my father's warnings, I was convinced Jay was a nice guy and even if he *was* a womanizer, that didn't mean he deserved to die.

There was something else stopping me from counting sheep in Dreamland. If Old James could kill Jay, what's stopping him from killing me or my father?

My hand trembled as I pulled my comforter closer to my chin. My father left my room as it was before my mother and I moved to Mississippi. I came home so seldom, I never changed it.

THE GROUNDSKEEPER'S DAUGHTER

Every time I walked into my bedroom, it was like I stepped into the past. The walls, along with my comforter and pillows, were all pink. In the dark, the color took on a reddish hue, that around this time of year should've made me think of Christmas but made me think of blood instead. I couldn't find how Jay's brother and father died, just that they died.

Compulsively my eyes scanned my room for the ghost of Old James, not that I had any idea what a ghost would look like. I hadn't pulled down the blinds because I was using the moon as a nightlight, but now I was thinking that wasn't the best idea. There were exaggerated shadows in every corner of my room. The shadows of simple, everyday items morphed into something sinister in the dark. My chair and desk, that I no longer fit in, morphed into something large and looming. The trunk my stuffed animals were stored in, shot up from the floor in a dark skyscraper. Shadows spread over the ceiling, stretching out like bony fingers. They surrounded me from above like a dark cage. I felt trapped, something I never felt before. Trapped in my room, trapped in this insane reality where a ghost could kill. Trapped with nowhere safe to go.

I wanted to sleep with the lights on but didn't want my dad to know I was scared. Because I *was* scared, really scared. My excitement over making contact with a ghost turned to fear the moment I read Jimmy Smith's obituary. I was the kind of scared you get after you watch a horror movie, where you keep looking over your shoulder hoping to find nothing. But if I looked over my shoulder, maybe I *would* see something and I wasn't sure if that was a good or bad thing but was leaning toward the negative. If I saw the ghost, maybe I could reason with it, but could a murdering ghost be reasoned with?

As the hair on my arms bristled, standing up one at a time, I wished I never clipped Old James's boxwoods.

"You're just cold," I lied to myself in a whisper, finding comfort in hearing my own voice. I was in a sleek red night gown. It was one of my holiday favorites thanks to the embroidered holly leaves and berries around the scalloped neckline. I like sleeping in night gowns, like the one I had on. It made me feel pretty. I know it's stupid, but it helps with my self-esteem issues. Home in Mississippi, it got chilly in the winter but not like Jersey winters. I was underdressed. The old cottage was drafty. I could feel the air coming in through the single pained antique windows.

I decided, in a moment of bravery, to shut out the moon, allowing my room to fall to darkness and hoping the blackout blinds would help hold back the draft. Hauling my shaking body out of bed, I reached for the string to close the blinds and paused. There was someone standing by the Smith monument. "Jay," I muttered to myself. Could it be him? The figure turned to leave. The moon captured his face, highlighting his person, it *was* Jay.

I rushed out of my room, not taking the time to put my coat on. I slipped my feet into my father's boots and was out the door.

I bounded through the snow, desperate to catch Jay before he left.

"Molly," Jay said, raking over me with his violet eyes that seemed light in the dark, which caught me off guard. If I didn't know better, I would say he was a ghost. His eyes had a reflective quality in the dark, adding to his already ethereal looks. "Geez, you're going to freeze to death!" He took off his coat and wrapped it around my shoulders, running his hands down my arms to warm me. "What are you doing out here?"

"I saw you from my bedroom window and was wondering the same thing."

He glanced back at the Smith monument; I followed his gaze. The peak of the memorial seemed to stretch upwards forever in the night sky. The sharp angles of the obelisk were lost to the endless darkness. The moon shone everywhere, but on the monument, as if the monument was a place of evil and the moon's beams couldn't penetrate it. I had never felt that way before, but I had never been out at night like this before either. There seemed to be no logical explanation on why that one place was showered in darkness while everything else was moon kissed. There were no trees or buildings blocking the moon's prowess, there was only the obelisk itself that smothered all traces of light.

Founder James had murdered his own son. Most people would consider that evil, regardless of the cause. Justification of that sin would fall deaf on most ears, maybe even God's.

"Your father found mine right here where we're standing," Jay said in a low voice that stayed mainly trapped in his throat. His eyes burned with intensity as they locked onto mine. "I was four when he died. I don't really remember him. It's more of an impression than true memories."

"I'm sorry."

He nodded his thank you. "My mother talks about him like he's still alive. It helps. It makes me feel like I know him. She adores your father, but I don't think she will ever take the next step because of my dad. She's stuck in the past. All these grave blankets are from my mother," he said, gesturing to the lush greenery that wrapped around the base of the Smith monument.

As a little girl, I always remember the monument being beautifully decorated for Christmas. I had always thought it was the monument's decorations that gave my mother the idea to make grave blankets for those less cared for around the holidays. Once I had even seen the woman busy at work placing the grave blankets around the monument. She was there with three young boys. It was Jay and his brothers.

"I come here to talk to my dad. He's not buried here; he's

buried at the new Smith and Stone cemetery up the street, but my mother believes when you die you leave a little bit of yourself in that spot. I guess I do too, that's why I come. It's my way to feel closer to him. I have a hard time sleeping and usually wander here at some point during the night."

"Does your dad ever talk back?" I asked, genuinely curious.

Jay gave me a sad smile. "Never. But that's not a bad thing. I hope he moved on. It's funny how you can miss someone you don't remember. I feel like there's a hole in my heart where memories of him should be."

He let out an exaggerated sigh, his breath coming out frosty. I knew he must be freezing. I was, even with his coat.

"I'm glad you spotted me," he said, his hand rubbing the nape of his neck. "Your father called me and asked me not to meet you tomorrow morning and I consented."

"What!" I said in a near shout. I was warming up quick, my anger making my blood boil under my skin.

"You can't blame him for not wanting you involved. He knows about the curse. He not only found my father but my brother. Jimmy's car was parked outside the cemetery. It seems like we're drawn to this spot to die. That's what was in the second letter from my mother to your father. Instructions on how to handle my corpse when he finds it. My mom's worried with his hip surgery, your dad won't be able to get around to well and she could be the one to find me. And she can't have that." He shook his head as if to reinforce what he just said, his hair falling over his eyes. He pushed his dark locks back, looking down at me through half lidded eyes. "We didn't know you would be here. All the same, I don't want you to be the one to find me. It has to be your father."

Tears glazed my eyes, blurring my vision. I felt like he'd already given up. "Jay, we're going to stop the curse. I'm not going to let you die."

"I hope you're right."

"I am, I'm seldom wrong, never in fact, ask my dad."

His grin spread. "Well then, I feel better already. And will feel even better once you get back inside. With a nightgown like that, you're sure to wake the dead. I don't want Old James stirred to life early and throwing tradition to the dogs."

I tried to suppress my smile. "My father did say you have a questionable reputation when it came to women. It might run in the family."

He laughed; his voice carried on the wind, whipping around the jutting headstones like claps of thunder. "Well, he's right about that. Bad as in nonexistent. I haven't dated since my mother sat me down with the letter from my father explaining the whole mess with Old James. To tell you the truth, I don't know how my father or my brother John could start a family. I wouldn't know what to say or not to say to my partner. Should I be honest? Do I keep the curse a secret and die without them ever knowing why? I just couldn't handle the responsibility of letting someone down. Sure, yeah, we're all going to die, but knowing when, the exact date, is mentally taxing, and on top of that the anguish of knowingly bringing children into the world who will share in the same fate. It was too much for me." He was back to rubbing his neck. "I admit I have a reputation of being a cold, insensitive jerk. It's not because I'm a jerk, it's because I'm *not* a jerk. I don't want to hurt people, so I don't let people in."

"I don't know about that," I said, drawing out my words for emphasis. "Just not showing up tomorrow after you said you would, sounds like a jerk move to me."

He sighed. "I would have called to tell you, but I never got your number."

"Not good enough."

"I know you mean well Molly, but what can we do?"

"A lot. I've been researching it all evening. Tomorrow, make sure you bring your birth certificate and social security card, we're changing your name. This changes the narrative. Old James kills James Smith. Well, by tomorrow you won't be a James."

"Okay, I see the logic in that."

"Then we're visiting the church to see if we can get a priest out to bless Old James's grave. I read you should salt and burn the bones, but the ground's frozen, so we're going with the priest option. Then I read rose bushes planted around a grave can contain an evil spirit."

He raised an eyebrow. "Really, how?"

"From my understanding, it's supposed to be symbolic of the crown of thorns Jesus wore during his crucifixion. Dark spirits can't cross the barbs."

"Okay. It can't hurt to try. I'm sure I can find a nursery that has rosebushes this time of year."

"I? You mean we," I said, clarifying.

"I meant I. Trust me Molly, you helped enough already. It was nice just to tell my secret to someone and have them listen. I don't want you in trouble with your father on my account."

I was right, I was the first person he'd talked to about Old James outside his family. A little fire burned in my belly at knowing this.

"My father leaves for therapy in the morning at nine. Be here for nine. He'll never know."

Jay was just about to protest again, when I noticed something moving behind him. I pointed, "What's that?!"

He turned. "What's what?"

"There!" I said, pointing again. I'm sure that wasn't much help. Thanks to the moon and the contrast between the dark headstones and white snow there were shadows everywhere.

"There," I said, my hand jerking to the other side of the cemetery. This time I saw what it was. It was a shadow in the form of a man. Someone was in the cemetery with us, and I wasn't sure if that someone was living.

I clung to Jay's arm.

"Hey, it's okay. It's just him."

"Him?" I parroted, my eyes searching the headstones for the shadow.

"It's Old James."

"How do you know?"

He nudged me, rocking me to the side. "I warned you about that night gown."

I couldn't smile, not now.

He moved forward, me still attached to his arm like a blood sucking leach. I was never letting go. "Let me get you inside, once I go, he'll follow me."

"How do you know that?" I asked, our crunching footsteps nearly washing out my soft-spoken voice.

"Since I turned twenty-five, I see him from time to time."

"What's he doing?"

"Waiting," Jay said in a solemn tone, his shoulders drooping as if it took a lot out of him to admit that out loud. "Don't worry, he won't do anything until Christmas. I think he's just keeping tabs on me."

"We should talk to him, see if we can't find out what he wants."

"Tried. Trust me, I tried. He never talks, he just watches."

I glanced behind me, looking for the shadow. It jumped from headstone to headstone like a dark flash of lightning, following us. With each leap closer it took, my pulse spiked. In all the years I had lived in the cemetery, I had never seen a ghost. The sight of its billowing form filled me with an oppressive dread. There was something inherently scary about the ghost being a dark shadow with no features—no eyes, mouth, or nose—just darkness. I knew it wasn't a trick of the light. The shadow moved with purpose, a dark purpose. Everything I thought I knew about the dead, was wrong.

"I'm scared," I told Jay, surprising myself. It was my way, to keep things bottled up inside my head because if I said them out loud it made them true, and I didn't want to be scared.

"Don't be. Old James is after me, not you."

"Are you so sure?" I asked, my mind going to my embroidered bookmark.

He didn't answer right away. "I'm sure."

"That means you'll be here tomorrow to pick me up, right?" I asked, having reached the doorstep. Jay's complexion seemed paler under the glow of the solitary porch light as if seeing the shadow had also shaken him.

I gave him back his coat, making sure to stand directly under the porch light, doing my best to give him a better view of my night gown as I waited for his reply. My nightgown, though sleek was nothing scandalous; nonetheless, it was low cut and form fitting. I didn't have the best figure, but I also didn't have the worst. And in the dim light, I was hoping it made me look better than I knew I looked in it.

I was beyond frightened and didn't want Jay to go. I wanted him to come in. All I needed was one little indication, just one glance down at the low cut of my nightgown and I would invite him in.

Jay had made the distinction that he didn't *date*, leaving it to the imagination what he did do to get a reputation. I knew he was a one-night-stand kind of guy. This mode of life was chosen so he couldn't get attached. According to him, not getting attached was for the girl's sake and maybe that was so, but I was sure part of the

35

reason he wanted to remain disconnected was to shield himself. Jay Smith was cold and detached and occasionally opened to itching that primal need. I hoped he had that itch now. Lust was masking my fear, and I was grateful for that. The shadow man hadn't taken the path to the cottage. It was waiting in the graveyard slinking slowly from headstone to headstone as if it was pacing. Still, it was too close for me. Whether it was waiting for Jay or not, having him with me was comforting.

Jay never glanced down. His eyes never left mine. There was something so frustrating in the way Jay turned me into a fourteen-year-old girl again, drooling over the most popular guy in school that you knew was never going to notice you. I was girl-next-door cute. My mother said guys date the cheerleaders and marry the girl next door. Not that that mattered to Jay. He wasn't into me like that and the realization of it stung worse than the cold that made my knees knock together. The more he opened up to me, the more I wanted him. Not just physically, that was part of it, but I wanted all of him. I wanted him to love me. He must do this to every woman he's met. Making them crazy, adding to his reputation of being a jerk.

Heat rushed to my face, my cheeks burning with chagrin. I was hoping, if he noticed, he would think my rosy cheeks were from being outside in five below weather without a coat.

"See you tomorrow, Molly," he said, his eyes so purple they looked like polished stone. "It means a lot to me that you would go out of your way for some jerk you just met."

Some people are special, just like Smith and Stone Cemetery is, but I couldn't tell him that. Instead, I said: "Don't be late," in a playful tone as I opened the front door. He flashed me a smile before heading back through the cemetery. In the warmth of the cottage, I watched him through the window as he made his way, stopping to look at the Smith monument again. It felt strange parting from him, like we were meant to be together. If only he felt that way.

CHAPTER SIX
A Turn of Events

I checked my hair again in the mirror. It looked exactly as it did the last time I checked it, which was less than five minutes ago. It was now 9:15; Jay was late. I knew Jay was going to prove a liar to someone today, I just thought that was going to be to my father. I really thought he would show. Maybe I was just self-projecting my own hope.

I had gotten up early and did my hair and makeup so when Jay didn't show at eight in the morning as we had agreed upon in front of my father, my dad would believe Jay kept his promise to him. That way it would be less suspicious when I texted to say I was going out with friends and not to expect me home.

However, I was beginning to think I was the one Jay lied to. I adjusted my hat in the mirror. With all the effort on my hair and makeup, I'd go out anyway. One can never do enough window shopping this time of year and I was down one festive mug. Retail therapy would make me feel a little less silly about dressing up for Jay.

I sighed, putting my entire body into it. I had wanted to prove to Jay I cleaned up nice and walking around with a cookie dough wort wasn't my regular. Oh well.

Glancing out the window again, my spirit instantaneously

lifted. I felt completely revigorated, like I just downed the world's strongest energy drink. My pulse quickened as the sound of my heart thumped in my ears. There Jay was, walking over the hill to the cottage. He was in the same long, dark wool coat as yesterday and walked with his head down. The sun crested his head and shoulders, highlighting the cinnamon shade in his hair. I glanced back to the mirror on the side of the door, smiled at my reflection, giving myself an approving nod before going outside.

"You're late," I said to Jay, marching up to him as if I never doubted he was going to show.

"Sorry about that," he said, his hand rubbing the back of his neck as he tried to avoid eye contact with me. "I didn't want to chance running into your father. I've been parked around the corner since 8:30 but then I thought, what if Al's running late. I was thinking, I should get your number before I forget, that way in the future you can text me when the coast is clear."

I was pleased he was thinking about the future. I spouted out my number as I walked ahead of him, we had lost time to make up for. He scrambled to find his phone.

"Got it," he said. "Sending you a text now."

I glanced at the Smith monument before we exited the cemetery from the walking path. It looked so different in the light of morning as if it and everything in the cemetery was at peace.

My phone dinged. "Perfect. Now that that's settled, where's your car?"

"There," he said, pointing to the candy-red Porsche, the key already in his hand. The car purred to life via the automatic start. Pop, the doors unlocked.

"How are we supposed to fit a dozen rosebushes in that?"

He lifted his eyebrows. "You were being serious about the rosebushes?"

"Heck yeah. I already called Jacob's Farmstand, and they

put them aside for us."

"I have a roadster, that may have a little more room."

"We'll make it work," I said getting in, not wanting to waste any more time. I felt like Jay's anxiety from yesterday was transferred to me. We had a very limited amount of time to break this curse.

"I thought the seat would be softer," I said to Jay as he buckled his seatbelt.

He smirked, a twinkle in his eye, "Come on, this car doesn't impress you?"

"No, not really," I lied, pursing my lips together like a sanctimonious snob. Oh, the Porsche impressed me alright, it would impress a blind man. I had never ridden in a car like it, and probably never would again.

"So, you'd like me more if I drove a rust bucket?"

"A smidgen more," I said, using my index finger and thumb to indicate an inch.

"I'll have to remember that in the next life."

"Next life—this life. When we beat this thing, you can give it to me as a thank you. This is more of a chick's car anyway."

He smiled. "And if we don't, you can still have it. I'll text my lawyer the addendum to my will."

"No need. Remember, I'm never wrong."

His smile widened. It was a nice smile, showing off his dimples. The Smith boys may be cursed, but they were blessed with good genetics.

***

"I can't believe that man! I thought priests were supposed to be nice."

It was the third Catholic church we went to and with Christmas Eve being tomorrow, no one could come out to Smith and Stone Cemetery to bless Old James's grave until after the New

Year. I had even offered, on Jay's behalf, a nice size donation if they could make it happen, but nope, it was a no go. I wanted a Catholic priest as the whole exorcism thing originated with them but was wondering if we should try a different denomination. Figuring I would receive the same response at any church, Catholic or non-Catholic, I ended up buying every prayer card Saint John the Baptist's had to offer. I also dumped out a jug of WAWA iced tea and filled it with holy water, which Jay found hilarious.

I was steaming by the time we made it to Jay's car.

"Hey, it's okay," Jay said, trying to calm me down. I was sure I looked like a raging bull with my hands rolled into fists at my sides and a heated scowl that made a woman pushing a baby stroller cross the street to avoid me. "It's not a big deal."

"It is," I said frustrated. "It's a very big deal."

The morning wasn't a complete wash. After a lot of waiting, Jay officially changed his name to Jay Smith. He refused to change Smith as it was his father's last name, which I understood. He hardly remembered him and the name was from him.

"Mol, like I told you while we waited for my name change, this has all been done before. I'm not the first Smith to change my name and we wouldn't be the first to bless the ground. My grandfather had even dug up Old James's bones and salted and burned them like you'd suggested last night."

I cut him an angry glare as I opened the passenger side door. "And you're just going to take it as fact?"

He got into his car, putting the jug of holy water on the floor behind him. "Yeah, it was all in the letter from my father. He outlined everything everyone has tried. And when I say everything has been tried, everything has been tried."

"Rosebushes?"

A smile teased at the corner of his lips. "No, no one has tried rosebushes. I'll make sure to write that down for my brother John, so his Molly doesn't ruin the interior of his Porsche."

My face wrinkled in confusion. "His Molly?"

Jay shrugged, before starting the car engine and letting it idle. "Yeah, the mystery girl Old James will send him to."

"If you think this is hopeless, why did you meet me this morning?"

"Hanging out with you beats waiting to die."

I almost smiled, that was until he held up his finger.

"There's a little bit of a bad boy in me. Your dad asking me not to see you, made me want to see you all the more."

"So, this is about pissing off my father?"

"And you—a smidgen," he said, mocking me from earlier, holding up his fingers, like I had done, to show me how little that actually was.

A loud sigh accidentally escaped my lips, forcing my shoulders to slouch as I cleared my diaphragm. It felt like a storm cloud settled over my head, pelting hail the size of boulders at my self-esteem. So much for the extra effort with my hair and makeup.

Jay evidently found me hysterical, throwing his head back and laughing like a mad man. His laugh was somewhere between hiccups and wheezing and was ridiculously cute.

When he was done, he glanced at me, his violet eyes seeming bright. "All jokes aside, I'm feeling optimistic about the rosebushes."

My eyebrows arched in suspicion. "Really?"

He nodded, a new smile teasing his lips that never quite broke through.

"Good," I said, my mood shifting. "So am I! Christmas is the celebration of Jesus's birth and roses symbolize the crown of thorns, it all kind of goes together."

"I think it's a great idea," he said, visibly biting back what I knew had to be a hiccup of a laugh.

I shot daggers at him with a cold stare that would've frozen the Heat Miser.

"Let's get to Jacob's before they close," he said, pulling on to the street.

* * *

"This is not going to work," Jay said, breaking his second shovel on the frozen ground.

"Duly noted," I said exasperated. I knew the ground was most likely frozen, but I thought we'd be able to dig far enough down to plant the rosebushes. "We're just going to have to place the roses around the grave. It should work. It's still creating a barrier."

"I agree," Jay said. "If it's gonna work, it's gonna work."

Jay arranged the rosebushes around Old James's burial plot while I sprinkled a huge container of Morton's kosher salt on the ground in the center of them.

"What now?" Jay asked, looking around the cemetery for my father or for Old James, I wasn't sure. I had been trying not to look around. I didn't want to catch a glimpse of either of them. I had done my best to block out the slithering shadow from last night and already texted my dad as planned, telling him not to expect me home till late. I hoped he was following his doctor's orders and was taking it easy, happily watching the television oblivious to what we were doing.

Jay's phone rang. "Let me get this," he said, having taken his cell out of his coat pocket. "It's my mom. I don't want her to worry."

"Go ahead."

"Hi Mom," I heard as Jay walked into the cemetery for some privacy.

I picked up the red gas can and drizzled gasoline over the boxwoods that just days ago I had spent so much time pruning. Thoroughly drenched, I put the lid on the gas can and waited for

Jay. I wished Jay would hurry up. Never before had I felt uneasy being alone in Smith and Stone Cemetery, it was my backyard after all, but I was cold. It was the same cold that had thrown the front door open after I had clipped Old James's boxwoods. And just like before, it iced me to the bone. The little hairs on the nape of my neck stood on end, the prickling sensation traveling down my arms and spine as my bones ached. I knew that meant Old James was watching, waiting.

    I tried to keep my focus on Old James's headstone, ignoring my peripheral vision. I reread the Godspeed message over and over again, recalling how I originally thought Old James was a friendly ghost after finding my lost bookmark. A new idea suddenly struck me. Old James had found my bookmark, my bookmark with my name on it, and unlike what Old James had done with Jay, leaving my license on his nightstand, my bookmark was left for me to find in front of his headstone. Maybe Old James did this as a way of telling me what he wanted. Maybe he wanted his name on his headstone. Could it really be that simple? Why else would he leave my bookmark there? He would have no way of knowing if I'd ever come back to his grave.

    Stepping into the center of the rosebushes, I went up to Old James's headstone. I ran my hand down the face of it, feeling for any indication that his name was once there.

    Jay approached. "Sorry, about that. I told my mom I'd stop by at some point today to see her." Before I could ask, "I said I'll see her tonight. Don't worry. I didn't mention your name, so it shouldn't get back to your father."

    I leaped over a rosebush in my excitement, grabbing his arm. "Never mind that, I got an idea!"

    "Okay," he said, his eyes brightening, "what's that?"

    "You should design Old James a new headstone. Look at

his stone, there's no name or date, nothing—just a message. I had thought time had worn away his name, but now I don't think so. I don't think it was ever put on there. Essentially, he was buried in an unmarked grave."

"Which was custom for criminals and murderers back then," Jay pointed out.

"Well, maybe that doesn't sit right with Old James."

Jay looked to the sky as he spoke. "Maybe it doesn't. Maybe that's what he's been trying to tell us." Jay locked eyes with me, a toothy smile blooming across his face. "Maybe he thinks his name *should be* on his headstone. Maybe he didn't murder his brother and wants us to clear his name."

My smile rivaled his, my cheeks hurting from my ear-to-ear grin. "You did say the facts were blurry."

Jay kicked at a mound of snow. "I don't know, Old James's ghost is without a doubt a murderer, so chances are he *did* murder his younger brother."

I shook my head enthusiastically. "Revenge," I said in a hushed whisper like a conspiracy theorist. "He's murdering out of revenge because he got blamed for a crime he didn't commit."

Jay raked back his hair. "Wow, okay, this is making a lot of sense to me. You could be on to something Molly." I could see the excitement growing in his eyes. They were dazzling purple now. He actually believed this could work. "So, all we have to do is solve a murder."

My heart fluttered at him saying 'we'. "That's not so hard."

Jay was back to sulking, his eyes cast in shadows by his hair falling over his temples. "We have less than two days to solve a murder that happened hundreds of years ago. I don't know, it seems impossible. Maybe we should just burn the bushes as we planned."

"Nothing is impossible, you have me. And I agree, we put a lot of effort into my rosebush idea and should see it through till the end. Let's light these puppies up and then we'll go looking for answers."

"Where would we start?"

"Um . . . you have any personal things that are linked to Old James, uh, family diaries or letters, newspaper clippings, or something like that? Maybe a family album?"

"No letters, not sure about an album. If we do, I never saw it. But we have ledger books. It's kind of like a database of business expenditures. If anyone in the family, including Old James, bought anything, it was written in the ledger. Maybe it could shed some light on what he was up to the week of his death. They're at the home office. It's not far from here. We've got to go there anyway to make the headstone, so it can't hurt to take a peek."

"There we go, we got our start."

"Okay, right," he said, his smile back, "but first things first." He pulled a lighter from his coat pocket, igniting the gasoline covered boxwoods.

"It's sad to see them burn," I said pouty. "They look so nice."

"They remind me of bonsai trees pruned like that," Jay said.

"I thought so too," I said with a sigh. "Well, I guess I should read the prayers now. And when I'm done, we'll put the boxwoods out with the holy water."

Before I could pull the prayer cards from my pocket, a gust of wind whipped around us, extinguishing the boxwoods and blowing my hat clear off my head. My hat landed in the center of the rosebushes. I reached in to grab it when I felt something cold grip my arm.

I screamed. I had no control. The shock of the bitter cold penetrating my coat was like nothing I felt before.

"What is it?!" Jay asked as I pulled my arm back with such

force, I knocked myself onto my bottom. Jay helped me up, locking his arms under my shoulders. "Are you alright?!"

"Something grabbed my arm. It was freezing," I said as my gloved hand ran up and down my forearm, trying to warm myself.

Jay was clearly worried. His eyes had spun little red webs over them. He took over rubbing my arm.

We heard the sound of footsteps over the iced snow. I thought it was my father, thinking he must've heard me scream and I'm sure Jay did too because he instantly turned scarlet. Together, we turned to face him. But my father was nowhere to be seen. The footfalls sounded again, the imprint of footprints marking the snow mere yards from us. There was no man attached to them, these footprints didn't belong to the living.

"Oh my goodness," I said, my arms wrapping around my middle.

As if kicked, a rosebush went sailing down the hill. Then the next. One came our way. Jay took my hand, pulling me back. I felt the sting of the scratch on my cheek before I knew what happened.

"We're sorry Old James," Jay said to the ghost. "Please, don't hurt Molly. I know what I have to do," he said, tugging on my hand.

I was so scared; I felt like my legs were stuck in cement. There was no shadow, no nothing, but Old James was there. I felt it in my bones. Jay yanked on my hand. I could feel Jay's tug, but I still couldn't move. I watched as rosebush after rosebush went rolling down the hill.

I hadn't realized Jay had picked me up and carried me to the cottage until he put me down.

He made himself my height, looking into my eyes. "Molly, are you okay?"

"Sorry." My voice sounded small to my ears. I had no control over my own limbs; my hands shook uncontrollably. I could feel the burden of tears lumping in my throat. "I'm sorry."

"You have nothing to be sorry about," he said, running his gloved thumb over the scratch on my cheek as if to assess how bad it was. He pulled my hat from his pocket and placed it on my head, brushing my dark hair away from my face. "You're going to be alright, it's just a little scratch."

"The rosebushes didn't work," I said, my tears finding release.

He took my shaking hands in his. "It's okay, it was still a good idea. Old James is a real asshole for kicking them like that."

I smiled. "Yeah, he is. They were really expensive, not that I paid for them."

His squeeze to my hands felt good—felt reassuring. "Molly, I'm sorry I dragged you into this. As much as I hate to admit it, your father was right."

I shook off my tears. "Come on, we better go before my dad sees me out here."

"I want you to sta—"

"Don't even say it Jay," I said, cutting him off. "I made you a promise and I intend on keeping it. Besides, I really want your Porsche."

He smiled softly. "You sure?"

"Yeah, sorry I acted like a baby. No more crying."

"What?! You're brave as all hell. The first time I saw Old James—" He paused to nibble on his bottom lip as if he was debating something. "I'm probably going to regret telling you this, but the first time I saw Old James, I peed myself."

The corners of my lips twisted up, silent tears still rolling down my hot cheeks despite my promise of no more crying. "No you didn't."

He nodded, as if that proved it. "I did. I was at my

apartment, watching the game and kicking back a few beers and then all of a sudden, I see this shadow standing next to the TV in the shape of a man. I was so freaked out, I flipped over the back of the couch and well, you know the rest."

I laughed; I couldn't help myself. It was the most animated he'd been since we met. I wasn't sure if his self-soiling story was true or not, but I knew it was meant to make me feel better, and that's what mattered. He cared.

"And as far as I can tell," Jay said, checking my jeans for a wet spot, "you did a hella lot better with this ghost thing than I did. Granted, I'm a seasoned pro after a few weeks of Old James popping in uninvited. But Molly, if you tell anyone what I just told you, I'm going to blame it on the alcohol. Right, that's what everyone does when they do something embarrassing."

I wiped my tears. "My lips are sealed."

"Promise?"

"Promise."

He winked. "Good. Now come on," he said, gently tugging my hand in the direction of his car. "Let's solve this murder."

CHAPTER SEVEN
His Molly

I sat on my hands all the way to Smith and Stone LLC. I didn't want Jay to know my hands were still shaking. He was right, the home office wasn't far, and we were there within half an hour. It was a nice building on the corner of Main Street. It had historical charm and was constructed of deep maroon brick, the kind you only see in old properties.

We parked on the side of the street and went up to the front door which read: Closed for the season. Two small and festively decorated Christmas trees in stone planters flanked the door. Smith and Stone looked oddly inviting for a business selling you burial plots.

Jay took out his key and unlocked the door. The inside was just as nice as the outside. There was a beautiful main lobby where I assumed Jay's brother, John, met with clients. There were scattered seating nooks around the border of the room like you would expect to see at a high-end hotel. Only the blown-up photographs hanging on the walls of different Smith and Stone properties hinted at why you were there. I smiled, seeing one that had my father's cottage in it.

I followed Jay past a room used to display coffins. I had no idea the Smith and Stone business encompassed so much.

"I work in the back," Jay said, taking me into what looked like a warehouse. There were uncut stone slabs in one corner and others that were finished and waiting for a buyer. Something about that made it look like an inside cemetery.

"Due to time, we're going to have to pick one of these for Old James," Jay said, gesturing to about a dozen different headstones. "It won't take long to add his name and dates. Which one do you like?"

"Wow, they're all very nice. You designed them all?"

"Yep," he smiled proudly. I was getting the impression he was more than happy to show off his work and I was happy to see it. All of the headstones were beautiful, and I was sure any murdering poltergeist would be happy with any of them.

Some of the headstones were more ornate than others, some were heart-shaped, others in the shape of a cross, and some in that traditional shape that comes to mind when you think of tombstones.

"Let's go with this one," I said, my hand settling on the rounded top of a headstone that had roses carved at the base of it like garland. "Old James is getting roses whether he likes it or not."

"Perfect pick," Jay said.

"Can you add Godspeed to it. I like the meaning behind the saying."

"Yeah, sure thing. I just have to pull the stone's measurements and enter what I want added to the computer, and it does the rest. It won't take long."

* * *

While Jay worked on Old James's new headstone, I went to the restroom. Jay had said there was a nicer one back in the main office, but I was fine with using the one in the warehouse. I didn't want to be too far from him.

I didn't want to mention it to Jay, but now that I calmed

down, I realized the place where I was grabbed back at the cemetery still hurt. In fact, it felt worse. I wanted to check it out in private. I knew Jay was ready to leave me back at the cottage after the rosebush fiasco and didn't want to give him any reason to take me home.

I went into the bathroom and took off my winter coat so I could push up the sleeve of my sweater. Any remaining hope that the dead can't hurt the living flew out the window. There was a deep purple bruise on my forearm. I could make out distinct fingers. I rubbed it, not that that helped.

I glanced at myself in the mirror. I didn't look so bad. My hair stood up surprisingly well for being whipped around in the wind. With my thumb, I wiped off my smudged eyeliner and evaluated the scratch on my cheek. It was small and shallow and would most likely be gone in a day or two.

I went to rejoin Jay, when something caught my eye. At first, I thought it was the shadow man from the cemetery, my pulse galloping at the assumption. My eyes registered black but it wasn't him. There was something against the far wall, draped with what reminded me of a black tablecloth. Fear was quickly replaced by curiosity. I looked around for Jay. Not seeing him, I decided to take a peek.

I lifted the black cloth and bit back a sob, dropping it to cover my mouth. It was Jay's headstone. The one he designed for himself. The date of his death was already inscribed. The headstone was designed with a three-dimensional Christmas wreath on the top of it as if he thought no one would come to place a grave blanket for him. I pawed at my fresh tears; I wasn't going to let this happen. I was going to fix this.

* * *

I found Jay in his studio, his coat was off and his gray sweater, that matched his eyes perfectly, was scrunched up to his elbows. A pencil was tucked behind his ear, denoting him as an artist.

"You like it?" He asked, gesturing for me to enter.

On a large piece of paper, that reminded me of a blueprint, was a facsimile of Old James's headstone including his name, birth date, death date, and Godspeed message.

"It looks great."

"Glad you approve. I'll feed the computer the order. We don't have to wait around for it. I already called one of my guys and he's going to deliver it tonight."

"Wow, perfect. I was thinking getting it to the cemetery was going to be an issue."

"We have a policy at Smith and Stone, working after normal operating hours earns you time and a half and an inconvenience bonus. This time of the year, everyone wants to be inconvenienced."

I smiled. "To the basement then."

"To the basement," Jay said, grabbing his coat. He paused by the door. "Hey, are you okay?" He asked, scrutinizing me with narrowing eyes. "Did something happen?"

"No," I said, doing my best to hold back my tears. The thought of Jay dying in two days made me want to breakdown.

"I think I'm just a little hungry," I offered as an excuse, having no idea what Jay saw. I assumed blood shot eyes and I knew I was trembly. In truth, I *was* a little hungry.

"Geez," he said, his hand going to the back of his neck. Which by now, I knew meant he felt awkward. "I'm sorry, I'm one of those people. When I'm busy, I forget to eat. "Do you want to go for lunch or an early dinner?"

"No. I don't want to waste any time. Do you have snacks in the office?"

"Yeah, in the breakroom."

***

"Wow!" I said to Jay as we stepped into the breakroom. "I don't think I've ever seen a nicer breakroom." Smith and Stone had one of those fancy coffeemakers that made everything and there was a wide selection of snacks on the counter in different baskets as if they were expecting a party.

"A lot of our employees have kids, and my brother's family practically lives here, so my mom makes sure we have a good variety of snacks for when they come to the office. Everything has to be from a peanut free facility, so it limits it a bit. Like me, my brother and his kids are highly allergic to peanuts and just about every other type of nut. We all have to carry an EpiPen."

I made myself a hot cocoa and went with a bag of chips. "That bad?"

"Yeah, that bad. If I'm being honest, I'm glad you didn't want to go out to eat. The whole eating out thing makes me weary. I have to stress to the waitress how allergic I am and explain that I can't eat something that was cooked in the same pan as something that had peanuts. Let's just say an EpiPen has saved my life twice."

"Oh my goodness."

"Yeah, it's no joke."

"Well, everything's peanut free here, so eat something. You must be hungry," I said, smashing a handful of chips into my mouth.

"I should but—"

"Try this," I said, dumping a chip in my hot cocoa and handing it to him.

His face twisted. "That's disgusting."

"Don't knock it till you try it. It's a poor man's chocolate covered chip. And yes, I know you're not a poor man."

He took the chip from me, over exaggerating his chewing. "Yep, gross," he said with a laugh. He opened his own bag of chips. "I have to get that flavor out of my mouth now."

"See, I knew you were hungry," I said with a knowing smirk.
"I guess so, being that you're never wrong."

* * *

Jay flicked on the lights to the basement, and together we headed down the steep steps. I held on to the banister with both hands to make sure I didn't fall forward. Old buildings like this always had steep steps and never failed to make me nervous.

"Too bad John already left for the day, I would've liked for you to meet him. I guess at my fune—" he stopped himself. "I guess another time."

My ears burned as another wave of tears formed at the back of my throat in a lump the size of a cannonball.

"John's the brains of the family. My mother always says he got that from my father. As brilliant as he is, he can be anal. Or maybe he's brilliant because he *is* anal. I don't know, I was always more of the artsy type. Funny enough, John has an obsessive-compulsive disorder that he sees a therapist for, and I think it's made it worse. But that's good for us, because you will never find an archive more organized than Smith and Stone's."

We reached the bottom of the stairs. It was a typical basement—cold and dank, despite being finished with drywall and a sealed concrete floor. The perimeter of the basement consisted of bookcases that ran wall to wall and were filled with hundreds of old books.

"Oh wow," I said, my eyes darting from bookcase to bookcase, "this is going to take forever."

"Nope," Jay said, with a smile. "John has organized everything by year then month. We just need to go to 1802, the year Old James died, find the entry for Christmas, and work backwards."

Jay went over to a bookcase, his finger dragging along the spines of the books. He stopped to read the spine out loud: "December 1802: Smith and Stone expenditures." He pulled it from the bookcase and held it up for me to see.

"Thank you, John," I said, beaming. "We'll have this murder solved in no time."

"Agreed," Jay said with an authoritative nod. "Let's head upstairs, the basement gives me the creeps."

* * *

Jay took me to the conference room. It featured an oblong table with cushy upholstered chairs on wheels. What I found most interesting was the timeline that ran across the back wall that reminded me of the kind you see at national historical sights. It was a timeline of Smith and Stone and the family, naturally beginning with Founder James. It had pictures and neat facts.

There was so much information on the Smith Family that wasn't available online. I wanted to read it, but Jay took a seat at the table and slid out the chair next to him for me to sit.

He opened the ledger and flipped to the last page. "This is an expenditure ledger. Any time something was bought it got written down in the ledger, along with the person who bought it. Here's how it works. As everyone has the same name, expenditures were denoted with the initials JS and their year of birth. It's how we still do it. Anything old James would have purchased, will have JS1777 after the description of the purchase."

"Got it," I said, my eyes already scanning the page.

Jay looked to the ceiling as if he was mulling over something. "This is the only thing that survived that still linked to Old James. I really don't know where else to look. There's a lot here so hopefully something will stand out like a firearm purchase or something like that and from there give us our next lead."

"I know it will," I said confidently.

His eyes reached mine and he smiled. It was different than the smiles he'd shown me before. It was as if he believed me. "Well

THE GROUNDSKEEPER'S DAUGHTER

Mol, no time like the present."

Jay and I scanned the last page, finding nothing out of the ordinary. He flipped the ledger back to Christmas Eve. "Now, this is interesting," Jay said, pulling the pencil from his ear to star a line in the ledger. "On Christmas Eve, the day before Old James and his brother died, Old James gave a loan of 100 dollars to Milton Stone."

I furrowed my brow in thought. "I don't get it, how's that interesting?"

For three reasons. "First off, this entry looks like it was squeezed between lines as an afterthought. It doesn't fit the neatness of the rest of the entries."

Jay was right about the handwriting. The penmanship in the ledger was impeccable, although you could tell entries were made by different people, all of the handwriting looked like computer font. This particular expenditure looked like it was scribbled in quickly and the penmanship was not of the same standard.

Jay tapped on the entry. "100 dollars was an insane amount of money back then and Milton Stone was Gregory Stone's only son."

I flashed a toothy smile, "Gregory Stone?"

"I'll show you," Jay said, getting up and going to the timeline on the wall. He pointed to an illustrated rendering of Founder James and Gregory Stone. "Smith and Stone LLC was started by James Smith and Gregory Stone. They served in the same regiment in the Revolutionary War. James took a bullet for Gregory. He survived his injury and after that James and Gregory were inseparable. Gregory was the only son of a farmer and when the war ended James went to live with him on his family's farm. You see, James was an orphan before the outbreak of the war and had no family. No one besides Gregory. Together, they decided to turn Gregory's land into a cemetery. Your father's cottage is the original Stone family home and Smith and Stone Cemetery used to be Gregory's farm."

I was fascinated by the drawing of Founder James. Jay looked very little like him. There was a severe quality to his thin lips and the set of his jaw, but Jay had his eyes. "No way?!"

"Yep. After the war, there was a great need for any and all funeral practices. Gregory had completed a year of seminary school prior to the outbreak of the war and due to the shortage of ordained ministers acted as a holy man during it. Gregory had made quite a name for himself, being charismatic as he was said to be. According to what my mother told me, he had become so popular that even after the war people were still coming to him and that's how it started. People needed to be buried, and they buried them. We still use Founder James's and Gregrory's business model today. Anyone who served and died gets buried in Smith and Stone for free and we offer discounts to veterans and any family members of those already buried at one of our cemeteries."

"I had no idea. I thought Stone was added to Smith because it was a cemetery with you know, headstones."

"I think most people think that. When Gregory died, James bought out his share of the business from his only son Milton. Milton Stone was known as a gambler and his bad habits and debts were affecting the reputation of Smith and Stone before Gregory's death. As soon as he could, Founder James bought Milton out."

I mused, "Apparently, he was still friendly with the family if Old James gave him 100 dollars that he most likely was never going to get back."

Jay nodded. "Stands to reason. Old James and Milton were close in age and I'm sure were brought up together. Milton ended up doing all right for himself in the end. He married the daughter of a chocolatier and helped with his wife's family business until his death."

"Six months after Old James," I said, looking to the dates on the timeline under the illustration of Milton Stone. "How did he die?"

"Suicide. John thought adding that to the timeline was tacky."

I honed in on the illustrated rendering of Old James. "Wow, he looks so much like you."

"Like all of us," Jay said, seemingly not bothered by me pointing that out. "Like I said, the Smith genetics are strong. My brother's kids are a year apart and they get mistaken for twins all the time and they look just like my brother as if they were cloned." Jay laughed his hiccup of a laugh. "I love those kids, but they're strange little guys, maybe they *are* cloned."

My eyes remained on the illustration of Old James. "I wonder what he was like. No one ever shared anything about him?"

Jay shook his head. "No. It was taboo to talk about him. Like his blank gravestone, he was erased from the family. By the time it was realized there was a curse, all stories of Old James were already lost to Father Time."

Jay pointed back at the ledger, "Let's see if anything else stands out. This Milton Stone thing could be something. It's a lot of money paid out the day before the murders."

"Agreed," I said, taking my seat next to Jay. "Milton Stone sounds like a desperate man with friends in high places."

Most of the entries were business expenses: ink, paper, wages to employees. Jay turned back a page and pointed: "Here we go, here's purchases made by Old James. It looks like he went Christmas shopping. Flowers for Mom, snuff for Dad, playing cards for James." Jay glanced to me, "This would be for the James, Old James supposedly murdered." He went back to reading the ledger out loud. "Teddy bear for baby James. Wow, would you look at this—Chocolates for Molly Reed. That's a strange coincidence," Jay said, itching his lip.

Dread twisted in the pit of my stomach. "I don't think it is. I've seen Molly Reed's grave. She's buried not far from the Smith monument."

His eyes narrowed, taking on a steely quality.

"Jay, she died on Christmas."

He spoke in a whisper. "Are you sure?"

Swallowing hard, I pushed my fear and tears down. "I'm sure. I don't recall the year, but I know she died on Christmas. Her grave always stood out to me because we share a name. As a little girl I always made sure Molly Reed got a grave blanket placed on her grave because it made me sad to know she died on Christmas. In fact, I put one on there this year."

Jay stood up abruptly. His chair sailed across the room, hitting the wall. He slammed the ledger closed. "Show me."

***

We made it back to Smith and Stone Cemetery at twilight. The sun was setting behind the city scape in the distance and the grounds were warmed with a yellow glow. But that was just an illusion. As we stepped through the gates of the cemetery the prelude to warmth and comfort were gone. The cemetery was still and cold. The shadows had just begun to peep from the headstones like phantoms.

Side by side, Jay and I marched through the ice-slicked snow. The snow that had melted during the day had already frozen over with the night's temperature drop. The sound of our footsteps reminded me of gnashing teeth. It gave me the feeling our presence was not welcome.

Standing in the ominous shadow of Smith monument, I pointed to the ground, to a small grave marker. "It's this one," I said, kneeling to remove the boxwood wreath I had placed there only yesterday.

THE GROUNDSKEEPER'S DAUGHTER

Jay gasped, sucking in air like he'd just received a body shot to the ribs. "She's part of this. She, like Old James and his brother, died on the same day."

It was true all three of them shared a death day. The stone couldn't lie. Molly Reed died at age sixteen on December 25th, 1802.

Jay raked back his hair with both hands before covering his paper white face. "Molly, I don't like this. I don't like this at all. I was teasing when I mentioned John's Molly, but what if it's true? What if Old James had sent Jimmy to a Molly. What if Old James is trying to reenact the past." He glanced at me through splayed fingers. "A past where—"

"Molly dies," I said, finishing his sentence.

He pushed his auburn hair back again, shaking his head at the heavens. "I can't even think of it. Dealing with me dying was bad enough, but now *you*." His eyes were on me. They looked glassy in the waning light.

"We can't know for sure if Jimmy ever met a Molly. The name could just be a coincidence," I said optimistically, hoping just that.

"It's like I said before, it would explain why his mystery girl never came to his funeral." He bit his knuckle as if to smother his need to scream.

"That's it," I said, anxiety building in my chest, tightening as if I was being compressed.

"What is?"

"If Jimmy met a Molly and she died, we should be able to find an obituary."

"That's right," Jay said, pulling out his phone. "You're brilliant."

We both searched.

I went to Obituary.com and searched all Mollys in the state

of New Jersey who died last Christmas. I sighed in relief before reporting my findings. "Nothing. If Jimmy did meet a Molly, she didn't die."

Jay slid his phone back in his pocket. "Thank God. I don't know what I would've done," he said, closing the distance between us. He ran his finger over the scratch on my cheek. He had left his gloves at the office. His hand was cold, but still I leaned into his touch, his hand now cradling the side of my face. "I don't know what I would've done," he repeated in a whisper, his soft words escaping in a cloud of hot hair. I inclined my chin to him, wanting to breathe his breath. He lowered his face, his violet-tinted eyes twinkled like stars. This was it—Jay was going to kiss me.

"Molly!"

We both turned at the sound of my father's voice. I could see him standing in the cottage doorway. "Molly, get over here now!"

"I should go," Jay said, taking a step back. He felt so far away now, like his one backstep sent him into a parallel universe.

"But what about Molly Reed?"

My father's voice rang through the cemetery, like a shrill bell. "MOLLY!"

"I'll go through the rest of the ledger and see if I can't figure out who Molly Reed was to Old James. Maybe she was his sweetheart. If there's more entries like chocolates, we can assume as much and from there—"

"MOLLY!"

"I have to get going to my mom's anyway. Text me when they deliver Old James's headstone, won't you?"

"Okay, I will," I said, not wanting him to leave.

He nodded, wasting no time heading to his car.

Running to the house, I turned back to see his silhouette cutting through the graveyard. He looked so lonely; I wished I was going with him.

"I thought I told you I didn't want you hanging around that boy!" My father boomed, before I got into the house.

"And I told you, you can't tell me who I'm allowed to hang out with."

"He's not nice, Molly."

"That's not true. I googled him. He's the most generous Smith in the history of Smiths."

"His charity is for show. He's just trying to make his mark."

My blood boiled in my veins at my father mocking Jay's wish to be remembered after he died.

"He's a Smith. His father was an asshole, his brother was an asshole and he's an asshole. And John's the biggest asshole of them all."

I had never seen this side of my father before. I didn't like it. "Drop the charade, I know you know about the curse. And does Jay's mother know how you feel about her late husband and sons?" My father's cheeks turned scarlet at the mention of Jay's mother. "If it's all true and Jay only has two days left, I'm going to spend them with him."

My father's voice was stern. "No, you're not."

"I am. You can be so stubborn, it's why you lost Mom. You better learn to compromise and quick because I'm telling you now, if you keep me from Jay, you will lose me too!"

I ran to my bedroom, slamming the door and locking it. I don't think I'd ever locked my door before. Throwing myself on my bed, my salty tears fell like rapids on my pillow.

* * *

A soft knock sounded on my bedroom door. "Mol, I'm sorry. Jay's not a bad guy, actually I like him a lot. He's always been respectful. His mother raised him and all her boys right. Jay and I have gotten close the last few months. He's been helping around the cemetery since my hips started acting up. It's just that I don't want you mixed up in all of this. I know you and I know you think that you can help him, but you can't. A girl showed up here with his father and his brother trying to help and . . ."

"And?" I said, unlocking my door and opening it a crack to look at my father.

"They both still died, Molly. I don't want whatever this is with Jay to affect the rest of your life. Jay will die on Christmas morning and there's nothing you can do to stop it."

I slammed the door and locked it again before free falling onto my bed in another fit of sobs. My feelings for Jay were consuming me. I loved him. I really loved him. I couldn't let him die.

CHAPTER EIGHT
A Visit

I woke up to a chill that climbed down each of my vertebrae like a xylophone. I had cried myself to sleep and despite having fallen asleep with my winter coat still on, I was freezing. I sat up in bed, my hand running the length of my arms, trying to create friction. I realized my top window sash had fallen, and the cold outside air was coming straight into my room.

Quickly, I walked around my bed, making a beeline to the window. I went to push the sash up when my eyes landed on an inky shadow in the form of a man standing a few feet outside my bedroom window. Instinct made me take a step back. As if sensing I saw it, the shadow man took a step toward the cottage. Until now, the ghostly shadow had stayed among the headstones, not venturing on the path to my father's cottage. I felt safe in the cottage, thinking the ghost couldn't enter it, but I was wrong. In what seemed like the blink of an eye, the shadow was climbing through the window, its form acting to blackout the moon. Just enough moonlight was visible to let me see the outline of it breaching the threshold. I thought my heart was going to explode. Stumbling back, I landed on my bed. Keeping my eyes on it, I crawled to the other side of the mattress, my unsure feet hitting the floor once again. Walking backwards, I found myself pressed against the wall. My voice was lost. Forget about trying to talk to it, I wanted to scream, but I couldn't. My trembling hand felt for my coat pocket to where I knew my phone was, my eyes glued to the shadow that stood in front of the open window. Finding my phone, I pushed the call icon.

"Molly, hey I—"

"Jay," I said in a raspy voice, hardly able to get his name out.

"Molly what's wrong?!"

My voice was barely a whisper. "I'm scared."

"I'm coming!"

I didn't respond to Jay, although I kept my phone pressed to my ear. I was distracted by the shadow as it took a step toward me. "What do you want?" I asked in a whisper. It didn't respond with words but with action, taking another step in my direction, then another, slowly making its way around the bed. With my free hand, I felt for the light switch. I flicked the lights on, thinking a shadow can't exist in the light.

Exhaling in relief, my entire body crumbled in on itself. It wasn't there; it was gone. My hands fell to my knees as I tried to steady myself.

Something was wrong. I got the feeling I was being watched. The weight of the stare was felt in my burning chest and compressed my shoulders. I glanced up, seeing nothing. Another wave of relief rushed over me, but it didn't last long. My eyes noticed something off, something just not right. The shadow cast by the bed on the hardwood floor seemed to stretch across the room. As soon as I perceived this, the shadow on the floor rose in front of me in the shape of a man.

I screamed, but the sound was trapped in my throat, only a gargling noise came through. I ran to my bedroom door. It was locked. I yanked on the door, putting all of my weight into it before my mind registered to unlock it. The door unlocked, I ran to the kitchen, turning around to see if it followed. I didn't see it. My eyes scanned every little dark spot in the room like a laser.

I wanted to run to my father's room or out the front door, but I couldn't move. I was frozen in place, stuck where I'd stopped running. Whatever had happened to my voice took over my entire body. It felt like I was trapped in ice, as if by degree, my body froze over, shutting down.

***

I have no concept of how much time passed from when I called Jay to when he got to the cabin. It was the dulcet sound of his voice as he knocked that thawed me out. I heard it, recognized it. As if by magic, the spell was broken, and my limbs were free to move. I rushed to the front door. Unlocking it, I threw it open. I wanted to run into Jay's arms, but I stopped myself, surprised to see him in slippers, pajama pants, and a sweatshirt. The perfectly manicured man I had come to know seemed so human. It threw me off guard.

"What is it?! What happened?!" He asked, pushing into the house. "Are you okay?"

"The ghost was in my room."

"It's okay," he said, hugging me to him. "It's okay, he's gone now."

My arms wrapped around Jay, completing our hug. He was warm, very warm. It felt good. In his embrace, I *did* feel like everything was going to be okay, as if he had the power to make that true.

"He does the same thing to me—spooks me, then leaves. He won't bother you again tonight. Come on," he said, releasing his bear hug and taking my hand, "Let's get you back to bed. Where's your bedroom?"

I inclined my head, "That one."

***

"No wonder why you're wearing your winter coat inside," Jay said, going to my open bedroom window. He pushed the sash back into place and locked it. This took attention to detail and brute strength to make sure the old brass fittings latched properly. I doubted I would have been able to do it myself. "It should stay closed now. These windows are charming as hell but not practical. I'll let John know to replace all of the windows in the cabin. You can't have the window sashes falling like this, you'll get pneumonia." He laughed to himself; a hearty stretch of hiccups filled the quiet room. "I just sounded like my mother."

His laugh added much needed warmth to the space, but the comfort was short lived as my line of vision fell on the view of the cemetery through the window. "That's where I saw him, at the window and then he came in."

"Not surprised. He likes to watch through the windows," Jay said, with a knowing look in my direction. "Regret coming home for Christmas yet?"

"No, not yet."

He smiled softly, a grin of all lips. "Good to know. I was worried you booked your flight out of here when you didn't return my text messages."

"You text me?" I said, looking at my phone I still clutched in my hand. "I didn't realize it. I fell asleep after I got home. I'm sorry."

Jay took a seat in my desk chair that was too small for him. "No biggie. I was just letting you know Old James's new headstone won't be delivered till tomorrow."

I took a seat at the end of my bed. "You find out anything about Molly Reed?"

"At minimum, I think our man was courting Molly, but I'm thinking she was most likely his girlfriend. He bought her chocolates every week. Unfortunately, she didn't pop up on any searches. John went on Ancestry.com and was able to find out the names of her parents. That was it and it wasn't helpful. The Molly Reed angle seems to be a dead end. John agrees with me that the 100 dollars paid to Milton Stone on Christmas Eve was strange. He's looking into Milton's last months. He wants to find out what the money from Old James was used for, though we're both thinking gambling debts. He had to leave my mother's after a while, the kids needed to tuck in for the night, but he's gonna keep searching. He's in awe of you, the entire family is."

"Me?!" I said, double blinking.

"Yeah, you. You put a crack in a cold case. Sure, it's a shot in the dark, but it's more than we've ever had. Sorry I couldn't keep you a secret. After your father spotted us together, I didn't see the point and didn't want to." He raked his bangs back, before rubbing his neck. "I hope I didn't cause too much trouble between your father and you."

"It's fine," I said, with a dismissive wave of my hand.

"I hope so. Al seemed pretty pissed. I felt a little bit like a coward slinking off earlier."

"Seriously it's fine. What else did John say?"

"He's hopeful, hell we're all hopeful, the Milton Stone lead will end this thing for good. Or, who knows, maybe you already solved this thing, and it will officially end when Old James gets his new headstone. If not, John has an entire year to solve the murder."

Hot tears beaded my lashes. "That's not good enough," I said, my hand balling into a fist. "We have to do it by tomorrow. Christmas is a wash. You're set to die Christmas morning, that leaves us only tomorrow."

He ran his palms down his flannel pajama pants, his eyes on his hands. "Molly, it's okay if we don't solve it. And it's okay if the new headstone doesn't appease Old James. I made my peace with dying. My life might be getting cut short, but I had a good life. I grew up with a great family and I feel like I did my part for the community." His eyes flickered to me, "And I got to meet you. I'm happy."

He winked, as if that was supposed to make me feel better about him accepting his death sentence.

I clenched my teeth to stop myself from crying. I could feel the muscle jump in my jaw; I was about to lose it again.

As if knowing tears were coming, "Well, it's pretty late and if we're going to crack this tomorrow, you better get some sleep."

My voice sounded haggard to my own ears. "What time is it?"

"A little past 2:00."

"I had no idea. I'm sorry I called you so late."

"I was up, don't worry about it. I'll stay in the chair while you sleep. For being meant for a little kid, it's oddly comfortable."

"You could share the bed."

"I'm good with the chair. I'm actually one of those people who can fall asleep just about anywhere. I used to get in trouble all the time at school for falling asleep during class. Besides, I want you to get a good night sleep."

* * *

I went to the bathroom to change, turning on every light as I made my way. I wanted no surprises. "Urgh," I griped into the mirror, "I look horrible." My curls were matted to the side of my head and my smudged makeup looked like a DIY clown face. Quickly, I washed my face and brushed my teeth. I wanted to put on something cute like I had worn last night but with my bedroom still frigid I knew I would come off desperate. In lieu of sexy, I put on an old nightgown and threw an oversized Mississippi State University sweatshirt over it and headed back to my room.

"Dressed for bed," I announced like a sports commentator, coming back into my bedroom. I peeled back my pink comforter. Even with the sweatshirt on, I was still cold and couldn't wait to get under the covers.

"What's wrong?" Jay asked, when I didn't climb into bed.

I just kinda stood there dumbfounded, my mind whirling, my brain not able to focus. "That wasn't there."

"What wasn't?" He asked, getting up.

I pointed to my bookmark and license that were on my bed as if they were made in it, tucked snuggly under my comforter where I should've been.

Jay picked them up. "You did a nice job on the bookmark. How old were you again?"

"Eight."

"Really nice." He put my bookmark and license on my nightstand. "Hard to believe you live on a street named Peanut Brittle. I thought the license was fake when I first saw it."

"It's a thing. Each street is named after a different sweet. I have a friend who lives on Cupcake Lane."

He smirked. "That's cute."

"I guess, but Jay you're missing the point. Why did Old James move them from my nightstand to under my covers?"

"He's just messing with you. He's probably watching us right now and laughing, if ghosts can even do that. He wanted you to know he was in your room to scare you."

"I already knew he was in my room."

Jay shrugged. "I wouldn't read into it. And hey, it could've been worse."

"Yeah, I guess he could have put a frog in my bed or a dead rat or something."

"Don't give him ideas."

I frowned, thinking I did just that.

Jay laughed, it was his normal good-natured laugh, but it didn't make me feel any better. "Come on, get in bed."

I climbed into bed and Jay pulled the blankets up to my chin like I was a child. I felt silly and as far from alluring sexy as possible.

I wanted Jay to spend the night in my bed with me. I knew it was impractical for two adults to share a twin-size bed and we'd both end up having a horrible night's sleep but part of me was thinking it could also be the best night's sleep curled up in his arms like a cat.

"I don't take up that much room. You sure you don't want to share the bed?" I asked, holding my breath. I was positive earlier that night, by Molly Reed's grave, he wanted to kiss me; I would make this easy for him.

Jay hesitated, nibbling on his bottom lip before he responded with a shake of his head. He went to the light switch and shut the lights off. The room was dark except for the steady stream of moonlight from the window.

My chest burned with embarrassment as I watched his darkened form take a seat on the chair. I closed my eyes to stop the tears. All the love I had for Jay wasn't reciprocated. I had read him wrong. Rejection sucks. I rolled to the side, facing the window so he couldn't see the tears that gushed from my closed eyelids.

"It's snowing," Jay said.

I glanced outside, my vision momentarily blurred by my tears. I discreetly wiped them. The snow was falling down in soft clumps that reminded me of the snow *from A Charlie Brown Christmas.*

Jay spoke in a soft tone that was close to a whisper. "It makes me happy to know it was you who put the grave blankets out every year when I was a kid. It always made Smith and Stone Cemetery my favorite out of our properties."

"I can't take all the credit. It was my mother and me."

"I always wondered why it stopped. I thought an old lady did it in her spare time and, well, died."

"Nope, just moved."

"You should do it next year and the year after that."

"I will," I said, sensing this was in some way his dying wish. My mind went back to his headstone I saw in the warehouse, to the carved Christmas wreath on it. It was beautiful but it was cold. I would make sure Jay always had one made with love.

"You promise?" He said.

My tears flowed unencumbered. I did my best to stifle any accompanying sniffles. "I promise."

"Good. No one deserves to be forgotten on Christmas," he said, mirroring my beliefs.

Jay Smith had my whole heart. I knew I could never love someone like I loved him. It didn't matter that he didn't feel the same. What mattered was my feelings. A ghost had brought us together and if I couldn't solve this centuries old murder, I knew it would separate us. Failure was not an option. I could live with Jay being my friend, I couldn't live with him being dead.

CHAPTER NINE
A Bittersweet Christmas Eve

I woke to a piercing sun. Its golden glare penetrated my foggy brain as I rubbed the sleep from my eyes, eager to get my day started.

Sitting up, I peered out the window. It snowed quite a bit last night. Everything was snowcapped, the snaking paths, the old headstones, the grave blankets. The sun made each snowflake twinkle like it was a diamond amongst a sea of diamonds, confirming what I always knew, there was magic at Smith and Stone Cemetery. It was as if last night was a dream.

At the thought of last night, my eyes fell to the Smith monument. For some reason it evaded me in the dark, but in the morning sun it shone bright as if the dark aura that surrounded it at night was never there.

"How'd you sleep?" Jay asked mid yawn.

I stretched my arms over my head like I was ready to take on the world. "Great. I'm glad you went for the chair last night," I said. I didn't mean it but acting like I did made me feel a little better about him choosing an uncomfortable chair over sharing a bed with me.

With a grin, "See, I know what I'm talking about."

"I guess you do," I said, rotating my body to face him cross-legged. "I was thinking . . ."

"Already?" He said, playfully.

I narrowed my eyes in what I hoped looked like an angry glare. "I'm always thinking."

The corner of his lip turned up in that cute way it did when he was trying to hold back a smile. "Thinking about what?"

"My bookmark. When I found it, I felt a mix of emotions, but fear wasn't one of them. Last night that shadow man scared the crap out of me, not as literal as your urination story, but it was bad and thus your presence in a chair meant for a grade schooler."

"Okay," he said, in a leading way, not able to keep the smile off his face.

"So, I was thinking, how at odds it all seems. According to the ledger, Old James, the day before he murders his brother goes Christmas shopping and buys gifts for the entire family including the brother he's going to kill. Fast forward a few hundred years and now he's finding my bookmark and license. Old James doesn't seem like the kind of man that would go out of his way to scare me last night."

"Death changes people."

"Maybe," I said, looking back at the Smith monument through my bedroom window, "but I think I'm letting hearsay influence my gut feelings. I didn't get a bad feeling at Old James's grave, until after you showed up at my doorstep. Maybe a strange feeling, but not a bad one."

"Okay, I'm biting, what are you getting at?"

"The other night, when I met you outside by the Smith monument, I got a *bad* feeling. I had never felt it before. But since then, I've noticed the monument seems to be shrouded in darkness at night." I put my hand up to stop him from interrupting. "Yes, I know at night it's dark, but the moon and the stars don't illuminate it. It's like a dead spot, no pun attended." My eyes honed in on him where he sat. "Let me ask you this, how did Founder James die?"

"Old age."

"Who died first, Baby James or Founder James?"

"Founder James."

"You don't think the ghost is Founder James, do you?"

"I think there're two ghosts. The ghost who brought us together and the one that wants to scare me and kill you."

Jay stood up, raking his hands through his hair. "Wow Mol, this is something. This could really be something. It never crossed my mind Founder James could be the one killing my family." His eyes cut to me. "But wait, why would he do that? Founder James worked so hard to build a family legacy, why would he do that to just kill us off?"

"There're two narratives: Old James is killing for revenge and plucking off your family at the same age he died at, or Founder James is killing everyone at the same age he killed his own son at. Honestly, if you'd kill your own son, what's a few great grandsons? It must get easier for him with each generation removed from the original crime."

"Geez Molly, this is nuts. I have to text John."

"Ask him about any and all dirt on Founder James. Not the PG stuff on the timeline back in the office. The stuff only family would know. Founder James was a very powerful man with enough influence and money to change the script to make him look like the good guy. We know he murdered Old James, but the handed down story paints Founder James as justified in doing so. I find it hard to believe Old James murdered his brother when he bought him a Christmas gift. There has to be more to the story. A lot more."

Jay pulled out his phone. "If anyone can find it, it's John. He and his family are going to Buffalo, New York today for Christmas at the in-laws, but he won't let me down."

I could see the excitement in his eyes. They housed the

same look he had yesterday when I suggested making Old James a new headstone. They seemed to glow purple. "Where do we go from here?" He asked.

"We consult the grave bible."

His eyebrows furrowed. "The what? Tell me that's not like the Necronomicon."

"Kinda. It's a book of the dead of sorts, but this one serves as a key to where everyone in Smith and Stone is buried. It's crazy old and sometimes extra tidbits about a person were added. There could be something added about Founder James or by him."

"Molly, you're really something."

I beamed. "Good thing I got that good night's sleep."

***

Jay and I headed into the kitchen to see my father sitting at the kitchen table with a book and his morning cup of coffee. The freshly roasted coffee beans gave the room a savory smell. I was surprised I didn't smell it from my room. It would've been a nice heads up.

Seeing us, my father put his book down. This was awkward. Living with my mom, my dad never met one of my boyfriends, not that Jay checked that box.

Jay wore a deep crimson flush, his hand rubbing the back of his neck. "Uh, Mr. Delray, um, good morning."

I couldn't blame Jay for the awkwardness. I guess it would be uncomfortable to walk out of a girl's bedroom in the morning to see her father.

"I, um, Molly was scared and called me."

My father stood, worrying me for a minute. I was clueless to how he would react to his *little girl* having a boy spend the night, especially since he wanted me to stay away from Jay.

My father extended his hand to Jay for a handshake, relief calming me, and I think Jay too. "Glad she called you. She's pretty ticked at me for the way I've been treating you. How about you come for dinner tonight. Molly's had her Christmas Eve menu picked out since before she arrived home. She's been promising me something special."

"Um, I, um . . ."

"Come," my father said in a stern voice that was more for show than anything else. "We both know your family does nothing for Christmas Eve and Christmas."

"Okay, Mr. Delray. Thank you."

"Al."

"Al," Jay said with a sheepish smile.

"Don't worry Dad," I said, feeling beyond grateful my father chose to embrace what he called 'my thing with Jay'. "Jay will be spending all day here. We have work to do."

* * *

After a quick trip to his apartment to shower, Jay returned looking very business casual and handsome. He knew how to pull off a sweater and dress pants.

"I'm making blueberry and banana nut muffins for breakfast," I told Jay as he hung his coat by the front door. Before he could remind me of his allergy, I corrected myself. "Without nuts. Let me start that one over. I'm making blueberry muffins and banana muffins for breakfast."

"Perfect," Jay said, taking a seat at the kitchen table. My father, coming from his office, placed the grave bible on the table in front of Jay.

"Wow," Jay said, taking a visible sniff in like he was a hunting dog, "that thing stinks."

"Nothing like the smell of old paper to wake you up in the morning," my father said, taking up his seat next to his cup of coffee. "What do you kids hope to find in there anyway?"

THE GROUNDSKEEPER'S DAUGHTER

I hated it when my father referred to me as a kid, but he did that to anyone younger than him. "Not sure," I replied, as I poured my second batch of muffin mix into the muffin pan. "Just anything Founder James could have written or anything someone may have jotted down about him and the same goes for Old James. If we could know for certain who the ghost is or *ghosts are*, it could make solving this thing that much easier."

Jay opened the book, familiarizing himself with how the key worked, and got to it. "Nothing on Founder James or Old James. Just the dates of their deaths, but I did find something interesting."

"What's that?" I asked, putting a hot plate of muffins on the table.

"Under Molly Reed, there's a cause of death. It reads: inflammation of the throat."

"What's that mean?" I asked, thinking I had never heard of anyone dying from inflammation of the throat.

"It sounds like her throat closed up," my dad answered.

I took my seat at the kitchen table next to Jay. "What would cause that?"

"Meningitis or Tuberculosis. Tuberculosis was a big killer back then," my father said.

"A food allergy," Jay said, eyeing the banana muffins as if checking them for nuts. He decided to play it safe and went with a blueberry muffin.

"Hmm," I muttered, taking a bite of my banana muffin and missing the walnuts. Having a food allergy must really suck.

Jay's phone rang. He got up from the table to answer it.

"Perfect. I'm here. I'll meet you outside."

He turned to my father and me where we still sat at the kitchen table, "Old James's headstone is here."

* * *

Standing between my father and Jay, I took in Old James's

new headstone.

"It looks good," my father said, breaking the silence that not only took over us but the entire cemetery.

"It does," Jay agreed.

Jay's design was beautiful, how the roses seemed to drip from the stone like they were mourning. I hoped this would appease Old James. If it was even Old James we were trying to soothe. I couldn't speak for the ghost, but I was happy my boxwood bonsais were still standing, flanking the new headstone. I hoped they would survive the fire and in spring new shoots would turn them green with life again.

I glanced at Jay as his gaze remained fixed on the new addition to Smith and Stone Cemetery. He closed his eyelids as if he was saying a silent prayer. But he didn't pray, he spoke to me in a whisper.

"This is it. There's nothing else. John texted me a while ago, Founder James was squeaky clean aside from the murder of Old James. And that was never public knowledge, only the family knew. He was a war hero, a good patriarch to his family and community, and well-loved and respected. If there was anything to the contrary, it was buried with the dead."

"There has to be something," I whispered back, keeping the conversation between the two of us.

"Nope. We're out of muffin crumbs."

My one eyebrow corked. "Muffin crumbs?"

"Breadcrumbs," Jay said, opening his eyes and flashing me a smile. "Sorry, I guess I still have muffins on my mind from breakfast."

"Jay that's it!"

His face screwed up, "What is?"

"That's what happened!" I took his hand excitedly. "I can

THE GROUNDSKEEPER'S DAUGHTER

end this."

"Well come out with it," my father said, just as anxious as Jay was to hear what I had to say.

"The chocolates Old James bought for Molly, they must have had peanuts in them."

Jay evaluated me with uncertain eyes as if he was considering what I just said. "Go on."

"I'm going out on a limb here, but I think Molly Reed, like the Smith boys, had a peanut allergy and didn't know about it. If she was dating Old James, she most likely stayed away from them. Something must have gotten mixed up and her chocolates were made with peanuts, and they all ate one, including Old James's brother, who according to family genetics would definitely have a peanut allergy. It would explain why they all died on the same day and would coincide with Molly's cause of death: inflammation of the throat. Founder James must have blamed Old James, being he bought the chocolates, giving rise to the rumor that Old James murdered his brother, and he murdered Old James. It was all one horrible accident."

"We already figured out why your bookmark was left for you to find," Jay said, looking at the headstone that now bore Old James's name, "and this would explain why I found your license. You live on Peanut Brittle Lane in Mississippi, MS—Milton Stone, the chocolatier. The ghost, the friendly one, was trying to lead us to the truth."

I beamed. "Old James was both the friendly ghost and the scary ghost, pushing us in the right direction."

My father scratched the side of his temple the way he always did when he was thinking. "If this whole thing was an accident, why would Founder James bury his son in a grave without a name like a common criminal?"

Because Dad, as we've seen too often with mourning

families, someone always has to take the blame. And in this case, it was Old James. Old James bought the chocolates. It was his fault and for that his father punished him.

Jay squeezed my hand, his voice breathless, "You did it, Molly."

"It's not over yet. The murders are solved but we have to clear his name. We'll post the truth online and with that Old James's name will be venerated and everyone gets their peace."

* * *

Jay had just finished his calls to his mother and his brother with the good news when I pushed post on the Smith and Stone Facebook page. I turned my laptop around, to show it to Jay. "It's over."

Jay had been flushed since I solved the murders outside. His complexion was rosy in the way young boys' cheeks turn red when they're playing outside. This crimson glow was a display of happiness. Jay seemed younger now that the burden of dying was off his shoulders and so very happy. His smile, not that it wasn't genuine before, now reached his eyes where his future burned bright with life. Words can't describe how delighted it made me to see him like this. I was right, this was going to be the best Christmas ever.

With dying off the table, Jay was quick to talk about his future, beginning with plans for Christmas, to which I invited him and his mother to the cottage, to which he warmly accepted.

It was a tradition not to celebrate Christmas in the Smith family, a point my father had alluded to. This made sense to me as it marked the anniversary of so much death and new death in his family. Jay's younger brother John went to his in-laws every year, trying to give his boys the most normal life he could; however, with news of the curse being broken, John was bringing his family, including the in-laws, back to Bloomfield to spend the day with his brother. I was excited to be starting a new tradition: Christmas at the cottage with the Smiths.

* * *

After dinner my father went to bed while Jay and I stayed up talking at the kitchen table. We talked about everything and anything, the flow of conversation twisting and turning until it ended up on my future.

"What are your future plans? What are you doing after winter break?"

My mouth twisted in thought before I answered. "I guess go back to Mississippi and continue at MSU. I'm registered for all different types of classes for next semester: Intro to Bio, Intro to Philosophy, Intro to Art, and English Comp II. I went in undecided and still have no clue what I want to major in."

It dawned on me that Jay wasn't the one leaving now, I was. In another two weeks, I would be back at classes at MSU, and he would be here.

Jay broke off a leg to the last gingerbread man on the cookie platter, his eyes seemly doing their best not to look at me. "I'd like to visit you. I've never been to Mississippi, who knows I might like it."

My heart fluttered, my full stomach twisting into a knot. Did he just say he'd consider moving to Mississippi to be near me? I was just about to ask him to clarify when the clock on the wall tolled. My eyes darted to it. It was midnight. It was Christmas morning.

"Merry Christmas Molly."

I smiled widely, "Merry Chris—"

The lights above the kitchen table flickered, accompanied by a high-pitched wrenching noise coming from outside. I gasped as if all the oxygen was suddenly pulled from the room. "It can't be," I said in a barely audible voice.

The shadow man was outside the kitchen window, his dark

finger tapping on the window producing a sound not unlike nails on a chalkboard. I looked to Jay, my vision already blurred with tears. "Jay, it can't be."

Jay stared at the shadow in shock as if it was the first time he had ever seen it. The color drained from his face. Even his lips lost their coral hue. His bright eyes went dark as if the flame that burned there had been extinguished.

Collecting himself, he stood.

I grabbed Jay's arm, "Where are you going?!"

"To meet him."

"You can't!"

He smiled down at me, his countenance one of sadness. "Hey, we tried."

"Jay . . ."

He slipped out of my grip and put his coat on.

I was on my feet. "I don't want you to go."

"Nor do I. But I don't want to get Old James angry. I don't want him scaring you again." He took my hand. "I will always be grateful to Old James for bringing us together, if only for a few days. As lame as it may sound, they were some of the best days of my life and I owe that to you."

I pulled my hands free, throwing my arms around him, doing my best to stifle my tears against his firm chest.

He caressed the back of my head, his hand running down the length of my long hair. "Thank you for being a good friend to a stranger who showed up at your doorstep lost."

I wiped my tears. I knew I couldn't keep Jay from his fate, and it was killing me. From his coat pocket he pulled out a ceramic mug. "I brought this today, just in case there wasn't a tomorrow. It's to replace the one that I broke. It's not as nice but I thought you'd like that it had a gingerbread man on it."

"Thank you. I love it."

Jay took a step back, aligning himself with the front door. "Remember your father's supposed to be the one to find me."

"I know."

"Promise me it won't be you."

"I promise."

"Goodbye Molly."

"Godspeed Jay."

He flashed me a smile and walked out the front door. I slumped to the floor sobbing. My love for him was overflowing, I thought that I would die with him. I couldn't let Jay die alone, like the others who came before him, alone and cold, and dead. I would be with him till he drew his last breath so he would know he was loved and that he would never be forgotten, not by me.

I opened the door and chased after him. Jay was already at Old James's grave by the time I came barreling around the house without a coat.

"Molly!"

I ran into his arms. He squeezed me to him, planting a kiss on the top of my head. "I love you so much Molly. I was trying to leave my mark on the world and that's not what's important. What's important are the little moments with people you care about. I never understood how my father or brother could start a family with the curse looming over us, but now I know. I hadn't met the right girl, until now. I wish we had more time."

I reached my lips to his. "I love you too, Jay." I said it out loud, so it was true. But I had known it was the truth from the moment he first knocked on the cottage door.

Jay's lips met mine in a soft explosion of lips. His urgency to kiss me made me weak in the knees. The tremble of his mouth against mine was bittersweet. I had never been kissed like that before and knew I never would be again.

We heard the sound of footsteps in the snow. We turned to see the shadow man.

Jay stepped in front of me as if to shield me. "I'm ready," he said to it.

"I'm not," I said, taking Jay's hand. "Jay didn't do anything wrong, please spare him. We gave you a new headstone and cleared your name. What more do you want from us?!"

"Choose," the shadow said. The sound of the voice made me quake. I was glad it hadn't spoken to me when it was in my room. I probably would've done worse than soiled myself. Its voice was deep, and it echoed as if its whole body acted like its mouth.

The ghost took a step closer to us. The ground around us fell into shadow as if this darkened figure was as tall as a house and with the dark, he brought the cold. The temperature dropped suddenly. Our breaths piped out of our mouths like chimneys.

The shadow pointed at me, then to Jay, before returning its dark, elongated finger in my direction. "James Smith, do you choose to save yourself or Molly? Only one of you will walk away today."

"That's the easiest choice I ever had to make," Jay said without hesitation. He glanced to me and smiled. "I love Molly. She lives, I die."

I squeezed Jay's hand, bracing myself. The shadow didn't approach us, rather it took a step back, growing lighter and lighter. The shadow continued to lighten as if a veil was lifting. Where the shadow man had been moments ago, now stood a sobbing teenage boy.

"Thank you, the both of you," he said, drying his tears on his dress jacket. "You've broken the curse."

The ghost wasn't Old James or Founder James, but the younger brother Old James was said to have murdered.

"All these years, I've waited for one James Smith to prove

he wasn't selfish. Every James before you was given the choice between their own life and saving Molly. In the end, they always chose themselves for one reason or another: I-just-met-her, I-have-a-family, I-didn't-do-anything-wrong. They all chose selfishly, like I had done when given the opportunity to save my own life or Molly Reed's. Christmas is a time to think about others, a lesson I had forgotten and was forced to teach my family from the afterlife.

"I loved Molly Reed since I was a young boy and thought we would marry one day. As we grew, it became evident she favored my older brother. I did everything in my power to prove I was a better match for her and the rivalry between Old James and I was born."

Young James seemed to get more real by the minute. He looked like a living breathing teenager as he wiped fresh tears. It was only the hazy glow surrounding him that hinted he was something more.

"When I found out he was going to propose to Molly on Christmas, in a fit of childish jealousy, I planned to murder my older brother. I paid Milton Stone an advance of 100 dollars to grind up peanuts and put them in Molly's chocolate. It was custom for James to buy her chocolates every week and custom for me to pick up the chocolates as I was errand boy to him and my father. I knew that Old James always snuck a chocolate before he gave them to Molly and Old James knew the same was true of me. My father would also take a piece. It was a joke amongst us that poor Molly only got half a box of chocolates because we ate most of them before she got one.

"As what was normal, I picked up the chocolates for Molly Christmas morning, along with the rest of Old James's Christmas purchases. I opened the box of chocolates to make sure you couldn't tell peanuts were made into the batch. I examined them one by one. Satisfied Milton did a good job, I placed the box of chocolates on Old James's desk and took my seat at my own, where

I watched and waited for him to eat one."

"We were only open for a few hours Christmas morning, just long enough to handle business. As you know, people die on Christmas.

"Molly had come into the office early that day. Earlier than what was expected, no doubt anticipating being proposed to in front of the family. She was dressed in her finest dress and looked like an angel on Earth. I had never seen a more lovely creature. Old James must have felt the same and gave her the chocolates without taking one. I knew Molly had a peanut allergy and if she ate a chocolate from that box, she would die. But rather than rat myself out, I let her eat one. I was a selfish coward. I'd rather let her die than expose myself as a murderer.

"What I didn't know, was that from my thorough examination of the chocolates, I had gotten peanut residue on my fingers. As I watched Molly take a bite of a chocolate that I knew would condemn her, I popped my fingers in my mouth, biting my nails in anticipation and triggered my own allergy.

"By the time Old James knew what was going on and fetched the doctor, it was too late. The doctor arrived and there was nothing he could do for either of us.

"My father pointed his finger at Old James. I had added the payout to Milton Stone in the expense ledger in the event Old James's death should raise suspicion. With my notation, it would look like it was bad blood between Old James and Milton that got my brother killed. Being aware of our rivalry over Molly and seeing the notation I added in the expense ledger, my father surmised Old James paid Milton to add peanuts to the chocolates to kill me. He, like Old James, knew I would have been the first one to take a bite of the chocolates and poor Molly got caught in the crossfire. He deduced Old James's guilt owing to the fact Old James didn't have a chocolate that day.

"From my death bed, unable to speak as my throat closed, I watched my father, consumed with anger and grief, force-feed Old James the rest of the chocolates, causing his death."

My hand covered my mouth. The truth was more horrible than I could ever have imagined. Poor Molly and poor Old James. Old James *was* the sweet and kind man I thought him to be.

"And Milton Stone killed himself over the guilt," Jay said.

Young James nodded.

"They all died because of me, because I was selfish. I put my wants and needs above others and proved that I loved no one, not even my Molly. Molly Reed was right to choose my brother over me. I was from the same stock as Old James, but I was not like him. With every generation, the Smiths grew more selfish, more greedy, more hardened. That was until Molly Delray melted your heart Jay and broke the curse that has haunted me and this family since I first plotted to murder my brother on Christmas."

I became aware of a man holding hands with a beautiful dark-haired woman in a dress behind Young James. To his side stood an older man. They were surrounded by the same yellow sunburst aura as young James. I knew the couple had to be Old James and Molly Reed. I recognized Old James right away. Jay and he looked so much alike they could've been brothers. They had the same hair line and jaw, the same violet-tinted eyes. The older man had to be Founder James.

Young James turned to them as a sob broke from his trembling lips. "I'm so sorry."

"You were forgiven a long time ago," Old James said to his younger brother before glancing to his father.

Founder James nodded. "Come home James."

Young James ran into the arms of his father. Old James caressed his brother's hair, still holding tight to Molly Reed's hand.

"Thank you, Molly," Old James said to me, his hand tenderly soothing his brother. "I knew, since you were a little girl, it would be you who broke the spell of Smith and Stone and unite my family. Thank you again and Merry Christmas."

Molly Reed smiled at me as if to say thank you.

"Merry Christmas," I said.

Old James focused his attention on Jay. "Life is short Jay, enjoy your new journey."

"Godspeed, to all of you," Jay replied, squeezing my hand.

Old James took his brother's hand and together the four of them walked off into the distance fading into the darkness. We kept our eyes on them until the sunspot disappeared.

Before I could say a word, Jay spun me around in a circle. I giggled with delight, my giggling silenced when his soft lips touched mine.

CHAPTER TEN
A Full House

The following year

We had a full house at the cottage. Everyone squeezed around the kitchen table where fresh cuttings trimmed from the cemetery were waiting to be turned into grave blankets. Jay's brother, his wife, and kids were over along with Jay's mother and my father. My mother and her boyfriend were there too, deciding to spend Christmas in New Jersey this year and I hoped every year.

I didn't have to worry about coming back to Smith and Stone Cemetery for Christmas because I never went back to Mississippi. I transferred schools and moved back in with my father. In the spring, Jay and I had a small wedding and moved into the cottage. With new windows, updated bathrooms, and a new HVAC system, Jay was as excited as I was to start our family in the home I spent the best years of my childhood in.

I felt a little bad about uprooting my father, but reasoned he liked living with Jay's mother better than being a confirmed bachelor. With the weight of the curse lifted, the entire Smith family was able to move on, including Jay's mother.

"Hand me the ribbon please," I said to Jay as I attached a Christmas ball to the grave blanket I was working on. He complied with a smile on his lips and in his eyes, planting a kiss on the side of my face.

    Against all odds, Jay and I had broken the Smith curse, but we realized there are some things we just couldn't break. We were having a boy, and we, like the Smiths before us, decided to name the baby James. In the spirit of the past, we decided to not only name the baby James but to call him that too. After all, I had never been happier, and it was all thanks to Old James.

    The end . . .

THANKS FOR READING!

If this book helped you escape, if only for a moment, please consider taking the time to leave a review or star rating on Amazon or whatever platform you use. It would warm the cockles of my little, black heart to hear from you.

Looking for something else to read? Don't forget to check out my other books on Amazon.

Follow me on social media (I'm on all platforms under Holly Knightley). Sign up for my newsletter for the latest news, glimpse into my wacky process, and occasional freebie. Stay spooky and happy reading!

WANT MORE?

CHECK OUT MY OTHER BOOKS!